QUERENCIA SPRING 2024

QUERENCIA
Querencia Press – Chicago Il

CONTENTS

POETRY

bloom – Antonia Rachel Ward (she/her)

take this blossom,
flush in its fledgling bloom:
this is you—
this is how i saw you first

dew-fresh,
newly budded,
petals opening as you turned towards the sun
r e a c h i n g

i wanted you

to press your velvet softness to my lips
and revive me

breathe life back into my crumpled years
arresting
the slow dissolution of entropy

everything i had wasted
you still had to come

i could buy an armful of you—
feed you, water you,
lovingly arrange you in a vase

and watch you wilt

It's more the being unknown – Maggie Bowyer (they/he)
—After Andrew Hozier-Byrne

I wake up, standing in the kitchen, sobbing. We are arraigned loosely, our chests heaving, the remnants of a fight tangible in each ragged breath. *Again?* I whisper. He simply nods and I wish, again how I wish. It never manifests; how can you use imagery and intention to create something you cannot envision? Something you could not recognize?

I settle into my couch, my cocoon, my cradle and my crypt. *Lonely*, her words escape their containment, *isolated.* I yearn, I ache in ways unrelated to my dislocated ankles and loose shoulder blades. I see the songbirds outside my window, taking advantage of the sun in the chill; I burrow further into my covers. Lonely, sometimes, but never alone, I remind myself as a squirrel busies itself in our garden beds.

Sometimes, when my lover's snore is audible, and the cats have accepted it is bedtime, I fantasize. I dance in the rain, unafraid of illness or ire; my mother smiles from the porch, not sulking or smoking; my father uses a gentle voice to call us in for dinner. I don't fight flashbacks in the middle of conversations with my fiancé; we live two hours from everyone we know, and we miss them, but not enough to give up the tranquility of the mountain sun. Sometimes we are homesick for the things we know, but we never feel alone.

This could be all we know of love – Maggie Bowyer (they/he)
   —After Gregory Alan Isakov

And I would be grateful.

My touch starved body arches toward your palms automatically. Your hands are calloused from hours in the garden and my fingertips knead the knots in your shoulders. You spill the contents of your day on my lap and I lay your head atop it. *Rest now,* I croon, feel me running through your hair.

There are years lost to me, but I know better than to go searching. Love is not found in that foggy forest. The past whispers, but you, my love, beckon. I come. I always come back home, back to you, back to reality, back to the path, back to myself. I always come back, and you are always waiting.

This could be all I know of love. This could be all I know of existing. Deprived is a word that comes up too often, but no longer describes me.

Please let this be all I know. I am so tired of knowing anything else.

Maggie Bowyer (they/he)

The words   *I'm dissociating*   get lost in the foggy forest
my fingers numbly thumb for the phrase
but the Raynauds makes it difficult
to hold anything close in this cold   *I'm sorry*
I let you down
and this apology crashes through the tree branches
but doesn't reach the sky   I know I'm getting worse again
I know I'm getting worse again
I know I'm getting worse again again again
I am tumbling through the underbrush
The main trail is swarming with screaming faces
in place of stumps   all the side paths have become overgrown,
unused after a harsh winter
I am scaring off every soft prey in my radius
I am terrifying myself   It is a frigid icy blizzard
I am stuck in
I am stuck stuck stuck

The words are stuck and I am standing in the kitchen
in the middle of the woods   and   I cannot tell you
I am screaming   I'M DISSOCIATING   but
I cannot make my frostbitten lips obey
I AM SORRY

You were an almost – Maggie Bowyer (they/he)
—After Amy Kay

1. I sat across from you at the coffee shop. We stirred forever into our mugs and blew ripples of regret across the steam.

2. You disengaged, detangled your fingers from my fists. I sobbed in my car while you banged on the window, apologies turning to sleet, bouncing across the pane.

3. We cuddled in the backseat. *This is the last time,* I lied. *This is the last time,* you promised.

4. Is every word the truth at the time, or are we all making shit up and hoping it sticks?

5. There are a thousand signs on an eight-hour drive, and I managed to ignore all of them. South Carolina soothed me with stretches of empty highway. Georgia screamed for me to turn around. Alabama wondered what I was doing so far from home, and I didn't question what that meant.

6. I am terrified of the things I claim to want the most. When I say I love you, it comes out as an accusation.

7. There is care within me, but not for you.

8. The drive north is a soft sigh of relief. I let heartbreak pick the music, and hope secured shotgun. The trip is shorter when you're listening. You were my shelter for too long; it is time to go home.

Is it snowing where you are? – Maggie Bowyer (they/he)
  —After Jean Webster

Are you headed to the cemetery to listen to the winter birds? How
is your garlic growing? When does your shift end? Planning to rest
the rest of the week? What are the kids' schemes for the season?
How do you intend to incorporate self-care into every movement?
Are the ghosts fogging up your windows? Is the dog snuggled
beneath the blanket with you? How are your feet? Weary? Upbeat?
Preparing to dance? Anticipating the global collapse? There is an
ache in my bones that could mean storms but it also might be my
body whispering it misses you; would you like to meet halfway,
find some cabin in North Dakota, and discover new ways to
unwind? Shed our exoskeletons and anguish? Start a riot in our
pajamas? If we can't meet in the Midwest, then what are you doing
tomorrow? Did it snow? Is the sky covered in clouds, or are we
looking at the same stars?

vice – Chriss Locker (they/them)

i.
it's the taste of your skin after you've cried
the tangles in your hair after a bad night
of sleepless-hopeless-endless searching
culminating in restless sex
that neither of us really wanted to have

ii.
i know better than to keep you here
because i know better than to think that
i'm the kind of person you deserve

because i see what you've become—
a once-vibrant creature of colors and lights
reduced to this bloodless being of silence
and i wish i'd seen the signs
but it's too late for that now

iii.
and baby nobody said this would be easy
this parting of ways and means and hearts
but nobody said it would burn this badly either
all the way under my skin
all the way down to the roots
where it takes hold and begins to whisper
you said you'd love her forever

*you said it and you _lied_*

iv.
we are both our own kind of broken
and i can't make your pieces fit
any more than i can pick mine up off the floor
but i still find myself waiting...
and i don't even know what for

so long – Maria Duran (she/her)

leonard cohen falls over himself—
dizzy with love,
so too goes our laughter
tripping down memory lane.
sunsets & leather seats: long childhood's
long summering. well marianne you left
& never did come back. so long! so long.
we shall go sit somewhere down the decades
& invent you some new memories.
don't be sorry, o muse. everyone has their own
song to die to. marianne never does come back,
marianne is out on the road,
hand raised to hold the sun, her own
summer's red fruit, hanging high.

Everyday I Dead-Shame Myself – Mattie-Bretton Hughes (he/they)

Monday

I dead-shame the tandem eyes that stare down at the bilateral form in the mirror. Reflection lies, I see them quarrel, try to convince me my heart can't pump for two unless there's someone in my womb. It's just an old pocket, an apron with strings attached to my soul where I keep all the dying stars. I can claw the skin but there's always more of me. I could cut it out. Make it like it never existed, but it did, and the hole that was there will be a void where I keep all the dying tears.

Tuesday

I dead-shame the dyadic orbs that point to me with a yearning for lips. A tiny mouth that will never exist. I feel them weep, yearning to give nourishment, colostrum, beastings of Mother Earth, and I refuse. I could bind them, tie them down like womxn have been tied to the ground since some man said the Earth began. I could have them surgically removed, twins of shame. The scars will be telling of a girl reborn into a body without a name.

Wednesday

I dead-shame the curves that flow around the form of me, like roiling waves, rolling hills over a vast terrain I'm unfamiliar with. Cellulite dips like karst topography, ample land, smooth as powder snow, decaying into fatty deposits. I could massage the flesh, force myself to touch parts only men have groped. Smooth the ditches where my blood won't flow. Age resists, dissolution persists, at least I can shelter in my own built-in spring. Worn away from the top, dissolved from the weak spot in my heart, pooling into orange-peel skin.

Thursday

I dead-shame the scars running like a road toward a life I'll never know. Tracks to nowhere, pits of burnt sins, bruises and stigma. Welts to remember the day I almost gave my life away. Notches marking each battle I disappeared into his eyes, died on the floor between his thighs, reanimated with the sun, when my battle's just begun. One line, a suture to the next, a patchwork of shared hurts joining together. A wound that I know how to heal.

Friday

I dead-shame the pain of temperance, my body marred in severance to reality, tranquilizing grief, dissonant tears receding into wood. Rigid, chronic spirit ache, I move in stop-motion, disabled to my vital child, mourning my mistakes. Now I drown in white paper reality. No one's coming to save me except twelve steps up a flight of stairs to serenity.

Saturday

I dead-shame the queer boy residing in my heart. Who will recognize that she's holding him hostage? He flutters behind a bone cage, chirps at crooning voices floating from the radio, nibbles at the flesh pumping life into my limbs. We danced in black holes, nebulous blasts expanding across sheer bifrost mountains, sprinkling over opalescent worlds. He pursued my breath like a comet, dazzling shock of a tail and mane sparking up the firmament. We lived a full life, burning bright, expanded, luminosity erupting one million times the size of infinity. Binaries, scattered far beyond origin. But infamy, before us, dogma void of life drawing our gravity to their event horizon, consuming our rays, one-third the speed of light. Their darkness sucking us into their vortex, every last drop of energy, until all that remained was the gaping abyss of our existence.

Sunday

I dead-shame the queer love resting on my shoulder. To carry the banner in this world is a dangerous endeavor. A blessing and a curse, and they could smell it on me. Ravenous boys out for blood, my soft bleeding heart. Victimizers on the hunt, patterned to generational bigotry. The blessing of a pure heart couldn't keep my body safe. Tender flesh cursed to the object of defilement. They sniff out unmarred flesh, and blacken their tenderness. Take bites of self-esteem, chew apart identities, grope the bodies of resilient girls and soft-hearted boys and call it games. Every night, I kneel at my window and pray my heart will stop dreaming for two. The world doesn't want our souls to bloom. Doesn't want tenacious girls and sensitive boys wearing hearts on their sleeves and taking up room. To carry the banner in this world is a holy endeavor. A blessing and agreement, a sacrament of heartsight, love, and mercy. Not for the faint of heart, but the ones who carry it freely on their sleeve, a banner the whole world can see.

I Am Death Beneath My Skin – Mattie-Bretton Hughes (he/they)

Stale sweat and knotted wood // he breathes me out like the wind // gone cold // gasoline burns me // inside I hear her scream // I distill grief in holy water // within the church of sin // The band plays on into my ears // mind blank of all fears // I am death beneath my skin // only he can catch me // before I reach Heaven // He watches me dance // in the void // in the nude // I don't exist here // except when his vo ce breaks the seal // My fingers // bone pickin' on strings // limp from strummin' // too much // strung too hard // strings pop // Heart breaks a flood // I taste love for the first time

Black Holes – Mattie-Bretton Hughes (he/they)

Do you know what it feels like?

When you stand there like stone, when you turn
your back, your mouth sealed and eyes cold?

A black hole.

Before you, I was bright as they came, a
nebulous blast expanding across sheer bifrost
mountains, sprinkling over opalescent worlds.

I was part of Heaven's Creation.

Before you, I was a star. Bright and blinking
and far away thinking what lay ahead of me for
this beaming life.

The noxious gas blasted off my cutting teeth,
blazing through the galaxies. Hotter than the
sun's flares, running wild high velocities.

Before you, I pursued my breath like a comet,
dazzling shock of a tail and mane sparking up
the firmament. I painted the cosmos with a
wink.

You'd better not blink, my presence won't
remain.

I lived a full life, burning bright, expanded,
luminosity erupting one million times the size of

infinity. A new star, scattered far beyond origin.

I rewrote History.

But you, before me, void of life drawing my
gravity to your event horizon, your heart,
consuming my rays, one-third the speed of
light.

Your darkness sucking me into your vortex,
every last drop of energy near me, until all that
remained was the gaping abyss of my
existence.

My light shredded into obsician ribbons,
hoover, compress, until I am less, until there is
no more to be. And you, alone in your
singularity,

Nothing. Nothing.

Just as before me.

Alcoholic Splurge And The White Light Dream – Mattie-Bretton Hughes (he/they)

The rain, it flows in my veins,

    I feel electric, drop my shell.

Throw my bottle at the fence,

    soaking my face in a backsplash.

Reeks of alcoholic splurge,

    I binge like a dream that won't end.

I dream in heat waves of white.

    White powder light, up my blood stream.

I've waited for, a dream, I've waited for...

    Moments turn to split seconds,

day into night, night into nothing.

    Black clouds cloud

the white innocence of life.

First published with The Argyle

Untitled – Irina Tall (she/her)

The lights are rushing, the white ones are swaying,

back and forth, flickering on the windows

bindings, looking languid

through the eyes of a freshly cut chicken...

Why did you leave?

I was disgusted by that reality

that I saw, people and what...

Everything around, everything that was like

into the sea, dirty and unnecessary,

tattered and broken and... Her hands

suddenly stretched out and she became

like a bird, turned into a white spot

jumped out of the window frame, and there she flapped her wings
and flew away

Into the distant clouds...

Spots float across green meadows

Turning the living into ashes...

Untitled – Irina Tall (she/her)

At dawn

By geometric slabs

In the semi-darkness of the door

Behind a wooden partition

Afraid to open my eyes

I will say: "live!"

And I'll plunge into eternity

Sleep, Where among the green lakes,

The whisper turns into a howl

On the scarlet disk of the moon…

There are a couple of swans that look alike

In the shade of large trees…

And I'm alone like a stone

I'm sitting on a thin white tree

With a trunk broken in the storm

And I think there's no need to leave

From where you feel good…

And the heart no longer beats…

Meeting the Seraphim – Archie J. (he/him)

Attempting to catch eye-contact with the many gazes of the
seraphim proves difficult
Bewilderment and slight terror overtake me

I'm forced to down cast my attention
Or else I might stare forever at this supposed horror

Oh, how to be a being who is misinterpreted
Supposedly, something entirely different than envisioned
Only to be a horrifying reality to those who do not understand

Yet, this how you always were

Forced into a mold that didn't fit the existence expected of you
Bound to be a frightening sight to those who catch your eyes

Forcing me to stare back, frozen in place
Unable to speak with anything but the plea of a line that I have
also spoken
"Do not be afraid; I mean you no harm."

Oh, I've been looked at this way as well
By those who are different
We are both victims of the cruelest fate

My eyes finally catching one of your many
I could almost be blinded by something that is the beauty of
difference

The misunderstanding of a being seeking only for my mutual aid
I shall offer you that;
"I give unto thee solidarity."

Wading Roe – Camille Colpitts (she/her)

Desiring Disgust.
Take, for example;

A bloody membrane rotting
vile scents immolating
leftover cum-purge rotations

save his hair & set it on fire with invocations
of desire
freedom slithers from
small cuts, bloodlust

tiny are these handmade persecutions

A French violinist plays a beat backed by house tracks
beauty begets disgust like a first crush
kept short & sweet
return to sender
lie with a stranger,
a baby does not know the mother is whole.

; the prodding nature of men en route to discover that the center
of the universe is an egg.

Salty – Camille Colpitts (she/her)

How wild are these winds?

Feathers joke and cackle at humans

Our salty wet hands

Catch tigers by their toes

Prayers divided by sums of possession

Rage causes the oyster to retreat

Futile are sorry fellows

While wildebeest consort with waging warlords

Water departs willingly never to return

The earth is a crow rabid with disease

Needle caps are the same orange as fire

Safety gauges coo on by the sound of pigeons

Those who are run over by the time dusk requires more coffee

Browning rats burn their feet on the tracks they cover

In due time we find our hands melting

But not before the fox finds us hiding

Gingerly by a snowdrift higher than our heads

Too little too late the whales sing while sinking sorrowfully

Looking for Datura – Fern (they/them/she/her)

I fell at once for the suggestion of your sound:

"I heard they pop just after dusk."

I used to carry my eyes through this land of hot red brick and mud,

that leaves no room for running silver,

only harder metals and eradicated opalescence,

stomped down the things that flower and shine

I used to wish moon beams, too,

would go this way—

leave their vines and trail away.

But I who left behind all these things that have pushed pause on becoming,

to find you, that scoosh—Your pop!— auditorily delicious, the lemon gaze icing,

your deep breathspace calling me forward.

This thing that would not leave me alone.

So I chase silver flashstreams

glimmers, swells, flooding his eyes,

you came out every hour: With your poison,

your beauty—how juicy to eat all of your deep breath.

In the soil where I park my bed on wheels,

next to the playground, edging moony paths—

all caught dusk and moonbeams,

children could eat you by accident.

My van pearly shines, you and I, glowing from the inside,

a splash of purple grief to hold close the aurora,

keeping just one eye flutter on the daylight hours.

Hiding away until nightfall, you sit still, insects riddle you,

passing through landscape fabric, my clothes torn,

I stay awake to drink this floral lunar glow,

And after a single efflorescence,

I sit in every aura's edge, every night—yellow street lamps,

zigzagging light of neon signs, running my tongue over glinting
teeth,

tasting Nightlight, quivers across rocks and rosebushes,

plaits juniper shadows over concrete.

Exhausted by dreaming lights,

With day break you curl up between the sheets of your petals

and go back to sleep.

I still have your kiss humming over my skin.

I know more than metaphor

and can leave hope alone for Daylight to make sense of

Colorlights at dusk: creamy yellows, purple written at your center.

You blinking, tipping in the wind, lips touching, a mouth closes

Time to listen.

You pop again, unfurling trumpet of night, chortling blessings
everything into being,
and everything else that floats in nightdreams,
reflecting in my eyes.

Curled into sheets you wrap around yourself
each day, all day,
spent at the edge of a window of light.

Saddling up to your eternal daydream,
dogs sleep,
wind ruffles your petals' edges
hiding away until nightfall.

I crave Nightshades in all seasons:
the Sweet darkness of greasy fries,
tomatoes halved by summer's knife,
eggplants roasted at the edge of a field.
You feed something else
this devilish desire to wake up without screaming,
everything silver.
You rogue in Solanaceae.

Candle-Making – Diane Elayne Dees (she/her)

I will craft a candle called Father,
with notes of whiskey, violence,
tobacco, and sawdust.
I will make one called Mother
with top notes of sun-dried sheets,
middle notes of freshly baked scones,
and bottom notes of suppressed rage.

The candle called Self, however,
will be my premium creation—
a hint of pine from the woods
where I hid from my parents,
a whiff of the delicate bergamot
and rosewood of my teenage cologne,
a suggestion of the bitter brews I drank
in countless New Orleans bars.

There will be complicated notes
of Bjork and Joni, melancho y
notes of Amy, a vigorous base
of regret, the lingering scent
of the essential oil of longing,
the sweet flower of wonder.

The candle called Self will fill a room
with scent that some might call complex.
It will burn for a very long time,
and then melt its bittersweet essence
into an eternal atmosphere
of unanswered questions,
a place where only acceptance
can keep the flame alive.

Something About This Day – Diane Elayne Dees (she/her)

Something about this day of flash floods,
dark rooms, small rivers flowing through
my yard, limbs down, emergency alerts—
something about this day of strange light
and isolation—something about this day
has made the food taste better,
the tears, more cleansing.
Something about it has made
the art in my house suddenly burst
into view, splashing yellow and red and violet
onto the walls of my waterlogged mind.
Something about this day has altered time
and gently nudged me into the present
moment, where I can float peacefully,
if only for a little while, until the storm is over.

Free therapy – K Weber (she/her)

Wherever a throat reopens. When
the chair supports every heaviness.

Legs dangle the day. An ear rises
to listen without music.

Yell in the direction of nothing
and then the refrigerator.

Open doors and flee, free, until
you arrive at the lake of sun.

possibility – K Weber (she/her)

i.
a hutch of green
glass in the same
small breath
as a sigh

ii.
fire lurking
the face
while the teeth
scream

Turnout – K Weber (she/her)

It was a cartwheel's
day: dew-dotted grass
met hands, feet; upset my

ankle. Bone had yearn
for mend. No stomach
for a yelp, no friend

to the end. Eyes winked
back at sky's eye, yawned
while the pulse cracked,

thunderous. Skin had not
yet green-grayed but ruddiec,
purplish. Rest entered, no

assist to stand. Wasp-
sharp stinging rattled
the buzz and poked

fun at the burn. The sun
too, laughed back
with a pinkened nose

promise.

Watering – K Weber (she/her)

My life is mostly thistle-
pricked, cactus-jabbed.
I strip my shoes and walk
barefoot on ryegrass.

If my skirt's short, blame
how nice rocket larkspur
feels as it licks my legs.
A slow countdown begins.

Spring blasts off in bold
italic: every color's tinge
gushing so I can eat violets
and hibiscus for dessert.

fortune glass – M.J.D. Deetzy (she/her)

someone has golden air
falling from their pocket.
and I unfold my fingers up to the clouds,
stirring the foggy stars, they puddle
and ripple like impossibly-still ocean waters.
the ripples turn to waves
and the sky becomes the sea,
above and below me.

my feet don't ripple the stars,
mosses and dirt and rocks greet me from above.
i'm underground, maybe i always was.

Yesterday, a yawn, half-satisfying and
Odious. crumbly rocks and dirt, now in my mouth,
Ubiquitous gunk clogging my throat of its tears. my
Scabs, i look at them
And try to
Imagine they could instead look like stars.
Delusional, they call me, but how right they are.
Yes, i am severely and dangerously delusional.

Once, i believed i could
Understand the fear, and was
Capable
Of banishing that fear
Under your bed, no matter how
Low to the ground that mattress sits.
Didn't you ever want to believe my
Nonsense as fact?
That wistful thinking and hoping that the very

Stars that glitter at night, would align, make
Everything seem alright?

Even this meager dirt is starting to weigh, and
Your eyes seem so distant now, your face, your mind.

Obliteratingly, these seas flood into me.
Unalterable, these demons, these shadows of lights,
Recidivism-like things, cold,
Suffocating, bright.
Eternally, enchanting
Laces imprinted into your skin, read them like
Fortunes on those silly paper strips, then
Maim them until there is nothing left.
Absent, now, of any coherent word, all, except the
Killings. you've done it again.

I've ingested the sharp edges of the strings,
Now decorating your skin in sepia-inked things.
Grainy glassed-over shards, glittering, freshly
Inked or blood-stained—only
The maker would be whom
To know. golds, silvers
Or steels, maybe, close its gaps. it's
Tarnished. which metal can't rust again?
Heavy-lidded soul-seers, yours, are in the glass.
Icky pools of blinded black blood puddle in them,
Restlessness dims my blues and other hues,
They ignite now, i think, though un-seeing, showing
Yellows of that new, burning moon.

*First published by Moonbow Magazine

Crystal Pond Monster – Michelle Gerlach (she/her)

Giant rough skinned newt

Who never grew up and left the pond

His mother's womb, like the rest of us

In fact, he's tethered down

An umbilical cord still attached like a chain

But made of...algae maybe?

That clings to his limbs in that shallow dusky emerald algae-
infested water

In that big pink newt, salmon color, like the great big fish he wishes
himself to be

He's got gills and a newt-like body, but he's been mutated

About 3 feet big, too big to escape on the little feeder creeks that
dribble down to that mighty

Willamette river on the big rainstorms and floods

When the ground is the slickest wettest mud he tries to make a
break again

That's the only time he works up the spirit, hauling that emerald
pond crud atop his gorgeous,

Pink, god-given but mangled and warped body

Sightings: two people have seen him so far, me and you

You can feel his presence when you come here

You can see his spirit, an eerie cage churning

Looming beneath a surface

Or behind eyes

Exposure to toxic methane gassing

I believe this used to be a holding pond

Note: wants to get back to the ocean like a salmon does

That's his reaction to salmon and his color

His color reminds him of that astaxanthin and the ocean

Note: check the article about old holding pond

For more info on the effect, eco-wise

Monster's peaceful dream

To be set free in the mighty Willamette

And to prowl and whack the banks as he sees the nutria, ducks and beavers above him

Wants wistfully to be like the great salmon

Note: something to do with the old Crystal Lake flooding

That occurred before dams

He is the last of his kind

Might be the last of his kind, actually

Locked bog monster Loch Ness

Homeland – Adonis Alegre (he/him)

You were so happy and yet, there was an excuse
happening in your memory that said, "I've never been a *homeland*
to somebody else, including my own,
yet I am nineteen and might not make it sooner,"
you stared back to the chimney,
"It came to the point that even silence was just a war having its nap,
that at any second,
there is a doom calling like the shape of a tree,
like a red growing thing,
that gown,
that death wore outside
of a prison, standing alone in a party it wasn't invited."

No matter how many swords in your pocket may be,
the great hold of one
is better than keeping many;
and this, I say to you, it has to do a lot with a lot of friends,
for an eye is an irony and a hand
is for sympathy
and I would call it a *sweet tragedy,*
trusting a sharp and nice human being
who had gone rotting its personality for money.

June and July – Adonis Alegre (he/him)

You waved your hand like a dead tree
bending on a windy *Thursday*.
All goodbyes that were never told are subsumed in the idea
of waiting and longing,
and some survived in the waves of that moving pond.
I have seen this in a dream of whims,
of where I would rewrite my diaries and hymns,
of how birds know how I sing your name
fairly and proudly in the morning of *June and July*.
Do some people thank themselves
for the things they didn't give?
Who knew I'd still want your soul to my soul, its other
wanting, its other half?
Who knew I'd still cling unto your dead and spared heart?

Almost as Air – Daniel Lockeridge (he/him)

Wraithlike, in outline
as well as lean, we are,
almost as doorways,
guided by doubtlessness,
our shoulders trailblazing.
Snowdrops not used to hands,
or cliffside passion
outside of self-dug ravines
of mere brushes.

Mere brushes help me
feel the air
as though it's creating,
from this side of the window,
with navy shutter-brushes,
in your gaze of smile,
while closing your pain.
I'm dressed in a stem-like comfort
while we're bare as everything.

I slide my forearms along
the growing bouquets
of your shoulders like shutters.
Our nerves become
dust, fabric—a must,
'til we are curtains, sheer-
snow in the new petal
of our living room archways
in the air.

Ultramarine Bars – Daniel Lockeridge (he/him)

Twigs are the above vault's veins
and I'm confident I can break through,
like you did on your home of bike,
or was that my quake-sized spirit,
when I was tree roots
dying like a climbing plant rising
as mere ether and evaporation
that had found its way
through my lava skin,
to ultramarine bars?

Music or support, each curl of sky
is flecked with soil's touch.
Body tiptoes to the first shoulder
of love that welcomes
an instrument, a distance
of transport seen from the bridge
upon which busker's tears
can't be heard or returned to coin;
we can't even rhyme as we flee
on squelching tires and swim

in soil, in time, but not in sadness,
because it's used up,
soaking into the roots that reach
the parks on the sun,
and in the core that consumes
you like a dream,
and on the other side of a world
that has broken into twigs
that we no longer put in the spokes
for a sunny joke.

One, Two… – Daniel Lockeridge (he/him)

Lightning doesn't spread between rose temples
to reduce to brevity her shouts to yarn walls.
Her voice continues to arch over her like a tail.
She watches passing plains from the passing garden,
pawing agapanthuses and placing the one sunflower.

She won't sleep, like all that is outside of the petal edges;
the enwrapping strings in which she feels like an edge.
The garden bobs into navy storms. She remains
the morning relaxed yet tense as the wall pulling her back in,
till she agrees to stretch forward and backward, a light bruise.

The stems, the strings, struggle under the sunflower, like mortar,
like air; like body-length feelings, rounded ends, the beginning
that goes on as long as two agapanthuses kiss
and a stranger tries to rub up against her—even her kicks.
She knocks down the strings and storms with lightning-hands.

Morning's drag – Grant Shimmin (he/him)

Where parallel lines of house upon house
meet perpendicular pavement
He stands, shabby bar slicked-down hair
Stomaching the morning through threadbare fleece
and the cigarette he guides seductively to his lips
holds tenderly, reverse-cupped, like he's cushioning a one-handed
catch
It's rush hour, but he has nowhere to rush to
Watching the rat race, whirling claws skittering on tarmac, long
teeth bared
Is this all the seduction his day holds?
Is the smoke the afterglow or is it the act?

*First published with The Argyle

The Droid Who Watches People – Mirvat Minal (she/her)

A passive aggressive fortune cookie once told me,
That self-awareness is a craft that takes time to master.
When I finally unlocked that secret level,
I performed a gamer's final level victory dance,
Before doing a "what do I do with myself now?" shrug.
Tin boots firmly on this red-tinted Earth,
Am I the only one aiming a custom-made spear out into the
abyss?

Apparitions of the yesteryears partially emerge from the corner of
my eye,
Renourished rising flowers of old gardens.
Delicate petal arms rise embracing the sky in a celestial bear hug,
A smile activated naturally via the mains in the pit of my chest,
To catch love would mean an excruciating short-circuiting seizure.
Everyone gossips,
Saying things like, "they're built different".
Yet cut from the same motherboard,
We bleed air.

Customised Manners – Mirvat Minal (she/her)

They've got endless simple solutions,
A backlog of remedial words queuing in their throats.
So, we nod to avoid further unsolicited consultations.
My people are a common alien species,
Classified as such by the world we're born into.
We used to be forced to stand in long queues like underaged teens,
Expecting to get in to an "It Club" whose music repulsed us.

I envy the residents of tomorrow,
But love the halted marchers of today,
We are the barrier's tenants, after all.

These consultants believe their tongues are magical forklifts,
That can scoop their version of us, out from our supposed hostage minds,
So they can empty us into a creamy golden pit of possibilities they puked out.
Like a carbon copy dish they'd serve.

The soft, sweet world they so easily digest,
Slides over to us as a bland dish,
And we're forced to use as many condiments on the table as we can,
To make our own world a palatable one for us.

Spirited – Ariya Bandy (she/her)

My worst? a siren in my ears I spawn
myself, but not

a hair on my head moves,
served on the bones of yesterday's me, the ringing keeping
me awake and asleep in the room / in my head and it's

noon, I've never made it that far
from my body, but I can't reach my remains, I see myself

scrunching the heated iron pillow over malleable ears,
might crush my skull to turn
it off, but we know I'm not strong enough for that, just one more
minute, each wrinkle in dust-housing sheets meets incompatible
skin, my hip sinking into the
mattress ready to absorb

me, and I'm ready to be absorbed, but why can't I just
get up? my heart is a paperweight only
holding down

itself. I rust behind the ears /
I'm not
even there to stop the song / my cells turgid with soot, I keep

scooping and searching for the problem
until my arm disintegrates into vapor / I never get
up,

the pillow suffocates me.

My worst? I can't
decide.

Peepal Tree – Ariya Bandy (she/her)

Sacred fig.
Here stands the kin of Buddha's place of enlightenment.

Your round
pointed leaves like soft-serve ice
cream. Reaching to the sky,
        hanging and supported
        by roots, numerous in span.

The air fires,
        bombs of rain
shots of lightning,
        and oh, how the wind
mixes, tearing away your branch, leaving
        its inhabitants for dead.

Resting in the grass, weeks without
answer. Part of the great healer lost.
Branch turned trunk—wood turned
chalk. Maybe a future as mulch. Today
I leave home, I come to say goodbye.

The tips of your fingers, beginnings of inflorescence.
Buds conceived in a flying
home.
A bouquet of cut
flowers brings one last blessing.

Multiple Choice for the Grieving Heart – Jess Whetsel (she/her)
  —After *Multiple Choice for Adrift Michigander* by Brian Czyzyk

How can one survive a season of grief?

    A. Surrender completely; allow yourself to be consumed.
        Eaten alive. Let it take bite after bite until you are
        nothing but bone and rotting scraps of flesh.
        Wait for the vultures. Wait for the wind.
        Wait for whatever comes next.

    B. Fill the vessel of your body with literally anything else:
        black curlicues of smoke, blood-red wine,
        midnight Taco Bell. Tell your bloated grief
        that your guest house is full. Let it pace
        outside your front door.

    C. Collect the empty bottles from the recycling bin,
        your grandmother's china that never gets used,
        a baseball bat. Take your brittle bounty
        to an empty field. Unhinge your vocal cords
        and scream at the darkening sky.
        Peer into the mirror of broken glass
        and fall for the feral glow
        in your bloodshot eyes.

    D. Imagine that your grief is a shrieking infant.
        Cradle it in your aching arms; croon a tune
        someone once sang to you. Resist the urge
        to shake it into submission; put it down and
        walk away for a moment, if you must.
        Return to its side when you are ready.
        Try to love it even while it is wailing.
        Whisper that you have no idea
        what you're doing, but
        you're doing your best.

As we float into tomorrow – Lizeth De La Luz (she/her)

i often think about the ocean / the rays / the echoes of subliminal
songs / the undertones of wishes / that fell holding on to /
weighted thoughts / waiting for them to disperse / to call out a
name / waiting for a body that will claim it / as a fallen / voice /
waiting to float / to fight the blankets of material / camouflaging as
space / as an abundance of a want / as a soundless plea /
remembering not the howl that burns / in suffocated dreamscapes
/ remembering not the undertones / of our surface / how we were
once water too

Pregnancy Tracker – Frances Klein (she/her)

This week, your baby is a lemon the size of a golf ball. A Boeing 747 the size of a hummingbird. Your baby is a blue whale the size of a bait herring. A neon sign the size of a light socket. A two hundred year old oak the size of an acorn. Your baby is an old growth forest the size of the preservation society's budget. A forty hour work week the length of a single evening. This week your baby is a multi-hour, cross department meeting the size of an "out of office" message. A time zone the size of a wristwatch. A library the size of a zip file. A body of work the size of a single pull quote. Your baby is an ever expanding, unboundaried universe the size of a postage stamp. Limitless potential the size of realized talent. An 8 lane freeway the size of the life in the rearview mirror.

Cain and Abel – Frances Klein (she/her)
—an erasure of page 269 of Steinbeck's East of Eden

you   kill your brother

for   want

you've tumbled a world

built around accepted truth,

a   pretty universe

You

cradled in the

fire.

You've been long   afraid

but at

the end there's light.

So

let

the evening come   let them

keep

your complications

let in

all the people who

came to the Promised Land

for a symbol

Basket of neglect – John Chinaka Onyeche (he/him)

"today's undone work is axed
into oblivion by the chores
that thud on it tomorrow
and spit it in the basket of neglect"
—Letters to Martha

Today, the world is blind-seeing,
the bloodbath traversing of history:
from her window, she watches,
the harming of her own before ideologies.
& she sat there, whispering, "defend;
defend yourself against your invaders,
& invade your invaders & defend yourselves,
where our humanity is questioned."
indeed, the world is blind-seeing.
if we neglect the lives of the innocents,
today it is Gaza, tomorrow it might be you:
if we keep basking in this basket of neglect,
the same was the genocide we called the Holocaust,
same we will be called by generations to come.
as of today, the world is blind-seeing.

Generic Horror Franchise – Elle Jay Snyder (she/her)

Someone is franchising the affirmations
you never said. They're writing a sequel
to my relapses. We go back to the same
mechanisms of torture. You crack open
my jaw. My words go unheard one more time.
I am sawing off your legs now. There's blood
everywhere—the disparate mess of my expectations.

We are making a movie. The same movie
we've made so many times before. It never hurts
less. But these sick fucks just keep watching. I'm cutting
puzzle pieces from our skin. They still do not fit.
I'm trying to dig the key out from behind my eye
but the director yells action. You tell me
you can't be with me. I push you in a pit of
syringes. You crack open my rib cage. I pour
sulfuric acid on your face. You pull my fingers
off while I'm electrocuted. I wrap you in
barbed wire.

And we both still say *I love you*.

The Storm – Abu Ibrahim (he/him)

My sister told me there's been an unending storm in her city. It's
been dancing around for days. Everyone has been advised to stay
indoors. A drunk wind had ransacked her city. It's been roaming &
leaving wreckage everywhere. Her city looks like a dump site, she
says. The roof of her home is twirling in the air and her apartment
is unrecognizable. All they can do is look up to heaven. They are
now hiding in the basement of a neighbours building. In the
basement, people are bent in the posture of a prayer. She's been
calling for help but no one is coming to save them. Nature cannot
be appeased when outraged. Over the phone, I sat quietly
listening to her speak, her monologue is soundtracked by the wild
howling of the wind. She lives in Middlesbrough and I'm in Lagos,
and I am still shocked by how she perfectly described the
meteorological report of my life.

Extinction – Melanie Hess (she/her)

rid us we must, this Goliath Beetle of oppression
we grab your horns and forked feet
to truss your legs and wings

never again to pinch, sting, maim and kill
or label and display us in resin and jars

our lanterns bright, you shall not lurk in shadow
exposed you look so silly: pasty, bloated, brittle

We will not arouse you.
We will not obey.
We rise, so many dancing beauties.

You would not survive without us.

**The Discrepancy Between Chronological and Subjective age –
Melanie Hess** (she/her)

I reek autumn
gelatinous
gravitational collapse startles birds and tourists

my soul is summer in everlasting bloom
a mango sun
briny ocean gush
rebellious hot pink bones

The Cactus – Cat Speranzini (she/her)

The cactus was a gift from a jungle cat that smelled of warm vanilla sugar with eyes as wild as storm ridden Caribbean seas and sharp nails that left half-moon crescents down my back.

I am not going to water the cactus. Not today, not fifteen days from now, not ever. I am not going to call the warm vanilla jungle cat.

I am going to curl up like hidden prey in the corner of this room and exit when the coast is clear. But then the kitten bats the cactus off the windowsill and it flies from its pot and lands on the floor.

So I move from my hiding spot. I scoop it up and repot it, pricking my finger, and a drop of blood falls into the parched soil as I return it to the windowsill. Blood magic, I think.

The kitten mews from across the room. I look at her, then back to the bloody cactus, then at the half empty water bottle still sitting on the coffee table. I said I would not water the cactus.

I have never been very committed to anything.

Untethered – Sarah Merrifield (she/they)

I'm starting to look more like my mother

And act less like her

I'm untethering the tether that ties us from birth

Birth means nothing

Death means everything

Untethered I become

My own entity I am not in her shadow

I am her shadow, her subconscious

The half of her spawn who refuses to endorse the sins written in
blood

She lives in a deep dark abyss

I am the light she cannot face

Lies that tear a family apart:

Where have you been for ten years?

What drains your pockets?

Why do you always have another home to run to?

What are you running from?

She's never at home

She builds tiny sand castles too close to the water purposefully

She self destructs,

And not only self

She destructs her tether

She reaches into the pit and pulls out my heart

I cannot imagine carrying a baby for nine months, then nine more,
then slowly,

Day by day,

Year by year,

Dropping them.

Your lies sprouted from the ground like weeds

There were too many to conquer

I was wrong about the fatal one

It was the tether all along, itself an illusion

"Mother" is an empty promise

"Womb" is a hollow home

For all the time we spent shackled together in the beginning,

You could never tell that now

I've had strangers show me more warmth

I was trapped in your body and my escape was a revolution

You love control; I was uncontrollable

You love facades; I am the truth

You bury your secrets amongst the dead

I am your shadow self

You cannot face me because you cannot face what you've done

You've accepted another casualty for your ego's war

There's no war

You're only fighting yourself.

Bears on the weekend – Elizabeth Adan (she/her)

you became a bear as you melted into the couch
and it was beautiful

that was last night
that was milk moon time
when the sky was pink and warm like crescent rolls

you say god has a beard when you come at my face like a lion
to kiss me dripping wet

I hear a car door shut on the streetcorner
and all those spoiled neighborhood dogs are barking
someone else must be carefree and delicious

the hum of noon
the frustration of 2pm
and the trains that no longer run

honey sweet
you're rotten and impatient
and I'm just here waiting for the weekends

you push me onto the bed and I can feel lace begin its ripping
and in this moment
I swear to god
that when we're done
I'm gonna stay up late tonight and pretend to pray

Time spent dreaming – Elizabeth Adan (she/her)

it's because your green eyes remind me of emeralds
and the woven copper you gave me by the waterfront
still sparkles sometimes

I love sourdough bread bowls and watching rainbow kites in the
wind
I kept having this dream
where we were eating sugar snap peas
and growing lemongrass in the garden
wrapped warm in avocado toast and high on happy music

I have an appointment with the morning window
to watch the ferries glide like knife blades across the frigid water

outside the dream
your sister is as breezy beautiful as a summer sunflower garden
and so is your wife
although not quite as much

it's because of the look you gave me in snowy november
because of how long it takes to fire roast a pepperoni pizza
and the waiting in between seeing shooting stars

I know exactly how much time I can spend dreaming
before my alarm goes off
and exactly how much jam you used to like on your whole wheat
toast

A Recipe for Postpartum – K.H. Belzer (she/her)

They had to cut all my babies out.
Cold scalpel sliding, a mouth of flesh—
a gaping portal nurturing a gasp.
A cry of arrival.

Psychosis comes in trembling waves, soft
at first, nipping at my elbows, tracing
warnings like fingertips on my scalp.
I always know it's coming for me after a birth.

A declaration, a becoming, a screaming
revival that calls a wave of psychotic fog to
visit, to sit with me in my blood, milk, sweat,
tears; it lays me down next to my child.

It spoons bitterness and hazy agreement
to my lips, tongue fuzzy with a new episode
of dissociation. Resisting just adds an element
of depression. Open up to the spoon.

Everything droops in a kind of bleak defeat;
postpartum belly like unraveled tissue paper—
lines, scars and tiny pockets that used to
host lanugo and eyelashes.

Womb trembles, confused and empty and grieving;
wrinkled gray matter inside my skull
doesn't recognize the person in the mirror
or the soul inside this body.

Prize – Ann Kammerer (she/her)

Mom went through
a couple jobs
and a couple boyfriends
before she decided
to move back to town
with my sister Janie.

She called
saying she needed me,
that she might
need Dad, too.
She had run through
all the money
she got in the divorce
and ran up credit cards
on a trip to Florida
with her friend Peggy.
She found out, too,
that lumpy nodes
were growing
beneath her skin,
lacing her neck
like a busted strand
of pearls.

"I been having chemo," she said.
"And throwing up.
A lot."

She broke down,
saying she lost her hair,
had to paint on eyebrows,

hide the withered purples
of her arms and legs
in Janie's baggy clothes,
her body a bruising ache.
A doctor gave her
fat white pain pills.
She takes one,
then two,
then three,
too many,
too fast,
too quick,
running out,
getting itchy,
her voice raspy
as she begs me
to go to the city,
to find those boys,
the ones who meandered
with white plastic bags,
ask if they'd sell me
a handful or more.

"You could do that," she said.
"Buy me some pills.
Get them to me.
Or call Shelley.
She'll bring them over.
She's always there
for me."

Mom got weepy,
saying that sure,
things hadn't been right,
that she'd been bad,
that she left me with Dad,

but that now,
she was different,
that maybe she'd like me,
that maybe things
would be good,
if I'd just do
this one little thing,
just once,
for her.

"You can do that," she said.
"You want your mom
to feel better,
don't you?"

She lit a cigarette.
I lit one, too,
remembering how
she tipped her head
and blew smoke straight up,
pushing her hair back,
saying something,
her lip half-curled,
waiting for me to answer.

"Yeah Mom," I said.
"I want that.
I mean I want you
to feel better."

I inhaled,
pulling the smoke deep.
She called me
a good girl.
Her cigarette crackled.

I blew out smoke,
swirls escaping
through the window
as I said no,
I couldn't,
I couldn't do that,
that I couldn't
call Shelley either,
that she'd have to
do things
all by herself.

"For Christ's sake," Mom cried.
"What's wrong with you?"

She wailed,
calling me selfish,
asking what daughter
wouldn't want
to help their mom.

"I sure raised a prize,
didn't I," she said.

Mom sputtered.
Something shattered
and she swore,
me hanging up
to the fragile stomp
of her feet.

"Does mental illness run in your family?" – Jillian Stacia (she/her)

No, but my great-grandmother taught herself to swim
just so she could scream underwater.

my aunts (3 of them) watered down
the world with bourbon—neat, no ice,

my sister washes her hands 17 times,
prays to the moon goddess, dances in the rain barefoot—
a water nymph.

my mother vomits up panic every morning
kneels in front of porcelain like some kind of backwards

religion, speaks in tongues to a god that does not listen.
she never learned to swim, never found a way

to water down all that rage. it crawls
up her throat every morning.

and now i can't stop screaming.

How do you love a man who begs you to kill him? – Emily Drez
(she/her)

The question gleams on the blade,
in the pulsing red of blood between my fingers,
and in his green, glassy eyes;
its breath cinnamon-sweet,
like the summer we spent between sweltering bodies
waiting for the other to pounce.

Letting a man go had never been so
                         easy, he pleads,
                              soft lips agape.
                                   How could you do this?
Licking the salt and iron from his argumentative mouth,
I laugh and croon,
You are so beautiful when you are submissive.

bombs – Niki (he/him)

i need 73 bombs
i don't want to hurt anyone
i just need 73 bombs
so i can keep them in my garage
or in the kitchen drawers
or in a pocket of my overshirt
when i have them i think it might calm me down
and make me a better person
both in and out
both with people and things around me
like, with the shoelaces and grass cutters and groceries
when talking to someone
i would be thinking about the fact
that i've got 73 bombs hidden somewhere
maybe close to my heart
or a belly button

hotdogeatingman – Niki (he/him)

pls send me down flying from an n-storey building
down to the ground you've sent me flying
flying is the motion through the layers of air
and this air makes an awful lot of noise in my ears
that's pretty unpleasant i must say for such a gracious motion

layer by layer you're closer to what people call dead
dead body or a murder or a bloody smudge on asphalt's surface
but once you've sent me flying what do you feel
what do you feel when I'm a smudge or a moody window

the man bought a hotdog downstairs in a proximity to the ground
and he was sitting there eating his hotdog enjoying it alright
but something hit the ground and splashed all this red nasty
liquid-y thing all over him
so he couldn't enjoy it anymore and wasn't feeling alright at all and
felt like screaming

it's my fault but i don't feel bad for the man or a hotdog
although i would like to cry and cry and cry
i wish i could enjoy eating a hotdog just like he did
obviously not disturbed and in complete isolation
from suicides or whatnot falls from the sky these days

i'd rather hide somewhere deep inside the city
where nobody would have access to me or my feelings
and eat a hotdog alone making a loud noise
chewing a lot and very slowly going through every bite
i will buy a thousand hotdogs and eat them all by myself
one by one

speed limits – Niki (he/him)

each season of the year flies into me on the same speed
the speed is approx. 200 mph
i think that's fast enough
to hit somebody to death or
crash the barrier with a car
so that the car would get thrown into the water
the seasons get thrown into the water
they sink with all the rotten leaves & trees & bushes & fences
squirrels try to escape but water fills their lungs and they die
i'm not sure how i feel about the squirrels
but i feel really sick because of all the stuff
that fills me up

mallrats – Niki (he/him)

it's me
who wakes up at 4:00am
and doesn't not know
how you look like
i can imagine you sitting in a car
in a parking lot of a shopping mall
it's Sunday 3:20pm
you open your mouth
like a fish
you open it
then you close it
then you open it again
without making a sound
if you won't make a sound
i might assume my ears went deaf
or i've died,
and i might freak out because of that
i might open the car's door
and start running
i will run many miles
until the realisation comes over me
or i would simply get tired
from running for so long
either way something happens
that stops me from doing
whatever i've been doing this whole time
i realise that i'm alive
i breathe and breathe and breathe

Blue – Emma Wells (she/her)

It had failed.

Coming alive to the wrench of bleach-washed floors, my eyes travel to bandaged wrists. Wrapped like presents. Above them, a baby blue sky, dotted with candy-floss white. Had I ever seen such a breathtaking view? Perhaps, my eyes used to be blinkered. Like a horse. Before.

A nurse wheels steaming urns of tea and coffee into the ward. Her squeaky shoes smile at me from a leathery darkness. I smile back. She takes it for an order.

"Tea or coffee, sir?" she questions, stitching a fake smile into the folds of her own face. I see the needle machinations churn behind her eyes. A rigmarole. The same every morning. Such a farcical display of meaningless goodwill.

Eyeing my safety-pinned bandages, her eyes flutter away; flares of discomfort tremble. Try to remain hidden.

Buried.

She feels sorry for me. A waster. A waster of life.

How could I do such a thing when a Monet-painted sky greets me from the open window? Summer verdancy flutters in, stirring the curtains like restless wings. I sigh, reminding her to cast a smile back into her eyes for me. Hope is what she represents. This will make her happy. This is the right thing for her to do, for me. A hare-brained patient struggling to cling onto slippery tendrils of life.

Teethed eels. Razor sharp.

How does she evade the fall? Run from the slippery suckers? What's her secret? I should ask her. She might coax my wrists, soothing me to unconsciousness. Dispensing like a pharmacist. I long for her invisible glue to reformat me. How much glue would she need to make a pretty portrait out of my fractured soul?

I dread to think.

She places a lifeless styrofoam cup on the bedside cabinet. Not wanting to touch my wounds.

The cabinet is brown. Not f eshed. Formatted like a soldier. Heartless.

She turns away. Done with me. On to the next.

My chance of fixing scars flies free—out the window, smothered by a hospital blanket of blue.

delirium Astronauts – Damon Hubbs (he/him)

under the firmament, we divide the waters
& add a day to the earth's rotation. It's love at first sight
or theia mania. Skyward we command the ship
write love letters in which every word is yes

our fingertips are crackling stars
& like John Donne we wear hats as big as continents.
We tilt & kick in apogee, levitate like birds in circuitry
write love letters in which every word is yes

we are stark blue nudes   hot Saturns   masters of revels
commanding the ship   til the sky spits the nipple
til hysteria   where did you go, my darling—
my atoms belong to you

A Wall of Noise at Vassar, '89 – Damon Hubbs (he/him)

We eat psychocandy and gaze at our shoes
long before you disappear to study British Romanticism
everyone incendiary with Frank O'Hara, us too
like a snake wrapped around an axe in Côte Basque

we put arms beyond use, fuse damage and joy
a wall of noise at Vassar in '89 makes our teardrops explode
we're lost children on the move
we're lost children head-on in love.

They bring soft axes to a summer picnic
dream of unpicking stitches of the galactic curtain.
Break it and take it until the goulash goes cold
like pigeons tearing a hole for the first crack of light

they have orange shirts with old-fashioned borders
but the sentry doesn't shoot.
Lorca plays guitar and the sentry doesn't shoot.
Everyone is on the move, head-on in love.

Arms Fair – Damon Hubbs (he/him)

feeling jittery around / contemporary architecture / is a sex act
—Ann Pedone

why do you insist on bringing me to these parties
and in flaming June no less
like an airshow   *kiss, kiss*   and I'm on deck
gown to ground at your defense expo

true, finger food at the arms fair
is to die for, and the viscountess is a crowd-pleaser
contemporary, but not new—
the party is her death bed

and she is sprawled exquisitely
in the sensual pomp of Nantucket's Pre-Raphaelites,
each room Gagosian, flowered and grand piano'd.
I watch your dick get hard

for an hour I pretend
to be somewhere in Switzerland.
You masturbate the heads of state
each contract like the best street in Amagansett

laid like an air raid in flaming June
the war mothers, and I
and the doulas armed with smiles
like Kalashnikovs,

my labia's fragmented planes   leaping lightly
a grasshopper of modern architecture
mechanomorphs,
like Picabia

I'm Thirsty I'm Dying – Alexander Beets (he/him)

My stomach's in knots, tied
tight from gunshots from
the driveway, burrowed
into the tree outside.

Me and Tom-tom measure our heights,
scratch the shrapnel shell, that fell from its
hole like acorns nesting in the cracks on
concrete sidewalk, into the side of

flaking bark on the great oak we called
Atlas. Atlas holds the firmament at
bay, his spindled fingers—I imagine
like mine when we brace ourselves

against the sky—how can I hold
the sky when I could barely hold
a pen. Ma' dukes calls it bold
when I make music through the night

to the beat of gunshots breathing past
the window, and the sparrows
the sparrows still sing their psalms
and eulogies in their wicker nests

and Tom-tom crawls into the
heft of my comforter head first, grips
the back of my chair; my kid brother
and his sobs sing their songs too,

his songs are like the sparrows',
somewhere between prayer and plea
and I learn, we are all musicians,
thirsty and scared and ravenous

and Atlas creaks when the wind
leans him towards us, taking the curve
of a mighty harp, he has come to pray too
and we all cry in our songs of death.

84

Wraith – Alexander Beets (he/him)

I used to hear the midnight
train from my bedside.
The whistle cuts through
darkness like the wind
cleaves with heavy hands
through our house.
We'd wonder if it was haunted
—if we could squint hard enough
to see the smoldering lantern
at the hand of the conductor.
Will he grin at us
with his ghost teeth.

The last memory I have of
Tom-tom isn't when he placed
the death-cold iron of the barrel
to his face and squeezed the trigger.

Nah, it was the same week our neighbor's
house burned down. From flames to ashes
before the fire truck could show. It was the
same week we snuck to the railyard.

Under the guise of night, he calls it the dream
train when it soars through the slanting rain,
ran straight to the glowering eyes
of the new paper mill.

He asks me if that's where my boy Ja' went
after he was shot six times in his back, stripped
of the sixty bucks and seven grams of pot
in his pocket. Eighteen years old and dead and broke

and without a proper fare for the midnight train.
Graffiti morphs on the passing railcars
And on the final one, slathered in rusted
white paint, is the word Wraith

and he asks me if that's
what we are. The train torpedoes
into the cascade of pouring night
and I wonder if that's all we'll ever be.

**It is the day of your death and I imagine The Madonna della Pietà –
Alexander Beets** (he/him)

I just finished rolling up outside,
sliding the curve of my tongue across tobacco wraps,
and at the flick of the lighter

the crack of a muzzle breaks
through my body, and before my
feet could move I'm sprinting towards

the house, and the acid in my throat
burns hotter than any heat off the
barrel. My knees buckle up the steps

and like the whistle of the midnight train,
I hear the cry of our mother through the thin
walls of the house; her cacophonous sorrow.

I stand in the doorway to see the
object of her horror; you
in her arms

and in your shroud of scarlet, I imagine
Michelangelo's The Madonna della Pietà,
son of Mary, limp in her embrace.

I imagine your jaw bored, like the holes in
Jesus' hands, hot nails still piercing. I imagine your
neck and shoulders slacked, praising

something other than the lord; and Ma',
her tears flow in the path of your blood
down the bare skin of your legs.

I imagine nothing is holier than the
tears of a mother who damns every
higher power—who damns it all

for her begotten son. Her sobs were
louder than the sirens of the men
who stripped her of her child, of the men

that pronounced him dead at 10:17 a.m.

I heard the train that night, left the husk
of my room and walked to the tracks
where I heard the wails of my mother
—the wails of everyone except
my kid brother. I took two of our Pops'
JP. Stevens issued gold pins

out of my pocket, and placed them on
The rusted lip of the dream train. I swear
I heard the sparrows still singing their death songs.

Crux – Alexander Beets (he/him)
—After Roberto Ferri's "Cupo Fuoco"

His coccyx atop the cool marble. Stale air ravages every chill on his naked body. Knees shake to stay up. Burs of his nails cinched into his scalp, each strand of sinew tugging on his fingers. Looks past his arm to the goat skull at his ankles. Clean, opaque, ready for mounting. He still sees blood. tacky. bitter. warm. Caresses its eye socket, feels the ridge of bone. dry. clean. not him.

Perching upon the lonely surface. Who dragged him there? Veins run hot across his serratus. Across every stretch of skin that darkness abandons, it only wants the parts it can use. So, he claws for what he can feel, what was once his. The air thickens on his heavy throat and his breath breaks against the moment's silence. And he knows that the narrow cavity of the goat skull is clean, so why does he still see blood?

FICTION

Adam and Eve File for Divorce – Addison Fulton (she/her)

In the end of the beginning, Eve says to Adam, "I want a divorce." She is the first woman to say this; she will not be the last. *Divorce* is one of the many words that flowed into her mind when her teeth pierced apple flesh. Other words included in the bunch were *lie, betray, alone,* and *love.*

God hadn't told Eve what love was because in Paradise? She didn't need to know.

"Fine. Me too," says Adam. He crosses his arms over his chest, *angry.* That's another one of their new words.

"Fine."

"Fine."

This is the first *argument,* the first *domestic,* the first *spat.*

"Why'd you eat that *fucking* apple?" Adam mumbles. It's a cheap jab that's meant to wound Eve's recently acquired sin of *pride.*

"Why did *you* eat the apple?" she asks in return.

"Because you did! So why did you do it?"

Eve runs her tongue over the little piece of apple skin still stuck. Residual sweetness lingers on her tongue. Even now— *especially* now, as the desert spreads out all around them—she could *really* go for a cold glass of apple juice.

The apple was *hers.* In a sense. Or rather, the choice was hers. How little was hers? Not the garden. Not her ribcage. Not her heart.

But the little piece of apple skin stuck in her teeth?

That's *for Eve.*

Even now, she can feel its phantom sweetness. The give of it under her teeth. Why give humans teeth for biting apples if she's not supposed to bite apples?

But she supposes it doesn't matter. Her mouth is *designed,* it seems, to eat apples, but she wouldn't have eaten it if she didn't want to.

And she had wanted Adam to have a little of what was hers, a compulsion because, at the time, she hadn't known the term *love.*

"I'm leaving you," says Adam.

"Fine! Good," says Eve. "You can do that now. You've got free will. So leave."

Adam stays standing where he is. His hands shift. Those hands are free to do whatever now, but they can't seem to choose what vulnerable place to cover first.

Eve covers her apple skin with her tongue.

"You leave," says Adam.

"What?"

"You ate the apple first. You leave. I'm staying here. You start walking."

"No," says Eve. She grinds her foot in the earth and kicks up dirt. "Why do you want to stay?"

"Why do *you* want to stay?"

"You think the garden door is going to open again for you, don't you? That's so *stupid,*" and Eve laughs the first laugh that has ever been laughed.

Adam looks away from her, up at the giant wall separating the past from him, "I want to go back."

It is the first hard truth ever to be spoken.

Eve laughs again—rage-filled, joyous sounds falling out of her mouth. The apple skin has driven itself deep enough into her gums that they've started to bleed.

"Well, I don't."

It is the first important realization to ever be had.

"We're going to die out here," he tells her. "I don't want that."

"Then why did you eat the apple?"

"Because you did!" he repeats. "Because I trusted you and I loved you!"

Eve's eyes run over him. His hand is currently protecting the spot where his rib used to be. Does she love him? *Does* she?

It's such a new word to her. It's so hard to define. Has Adam defined it? What does he mean?

"I want to be free."

"I want to be safe."

They are having the first disagreement. They are having one of the oldest.

"It appears we've hit a wall," Eve says. She stares up at the first wall. It separates her from everything she's ever known. It shoves her toward everything that one day will be known. The whole, horrible world stretches out beyond her.

"It appears we have."

"Then we should go different ways."

They come to the first agreement.

"You'll go that way," Eve says. "And I'll go that way."

"And if we ever see each other again, we'll pretend we don't know each other."

And yet neither moves. They could. They have their free will, now. They are their own to control. And yet—

"Did you hear that, God?" Eve yells into the sky. It is so big, now. The leering eye of the sun is unhidden by flowers and fruit trees. She knows they're being watched. "We want a divorce. We want to be separate now."

God doesn't answer them. Instead, He sends ravens and vultures to circle overhead, waiting. Wolves prowl nearby. *These* creatures God has gifted the ability to mate for life. He has granted them mercy and community. Simplicity. No apples for the vultures and the ravens.

They survive in pairs and packs.

"We're free now," Eve says. It is a horrible thing for a human to know.

"We stand a better chance of surviving if we stick together," Adam says. It is a horrible thing to know.

"I *chose* to eat the apple," Eve says.

"I know."

"I'm not in love with you."

"I know," Adam says.

"I didn't choose to be here."

"I know."

"I didn't *choose* to be your wife."

"I know."

The birds. The wolves. The sun. Beauty and death and love are all around them. Birds and wolves are less controlled by God. They choose their own mates. They choose their mates in order to survive, in order to make their children survive. They choose, but they have to. This is how they live.

"I love you," Eve says.

"I love you too."

"I have no choice."

"You do," Adam says. The birds and the wolves press closer. The first humans huddle closer to each other. "You could choose to die."

"I could."

"But you won't?"

"But I won't."

Adam nods. He tips his head up toward the sky.

"I think that's a good choice."

96

The Art House – Addison Fulton (she/her)

The most recent exhibit at The Arthouse, John's art gallery, is a series that the artist painted in her own blood. It's a statement, the placard explains, on the inherent vulnerability of creating art. It's a bearing of the soul, of the self. Most of the paintings are bloody still-lifes of pomegranates and roses.

John stares at them, watching people mill about, gawking and examining and pondering. The exhibit brought in good money. The press was alarmed, wondering if modern art had gone too far. They wanted to go back to the good old days of the *Mona Lisa*, or at least the comfortable, bad old days of bananas stapled to the wall.

But the people were curious.

Is this the soul? Is it made of blood? Hamlet claimed art was a mirror. Was this the mirror? Is this *his* soul?

John used to want to *make* art, but found himself unhappy with everything he made. So, to stay close to art, he opened The Arthouse instead.

It's hard to see in a mirror so covered in blood.

No. This couldn't be it.

The Arthouse used to showcase normal art until John's mother died. It was a car crash, a bad one. Fiery. The mortician did the best they could for her corpse, but her will had called explicitly for an open casket. Even under the wig they gave her, John had to see the part where her skull was open and her brain had been removed. He was staring at the open void where all her memories and personality had been but couldn't comprehend it. It was then he realized that the soul couldn't live in the brain where it could be so easily removed. It had to live elsewhere. Like the Greeks and Victorians and other less-than-scientific, more-than-artistic societies had believed.

The Arthouse's next exhibit was called *Arete/Catharsis*. It featured a woman laughing for two hours straight, and then sobbing for two hours straight.

It was performance art.

It didn't help John find the soul.

The current exhibit, the one with the blood and the pomegranates, wasn't helping either.

Dr. Doe has recently been sued for malpractice and lost his job. He was arrested for selling people surgeries they didn't really need. The surgery was expensive, but so is medical school. What goes around comes around.

Privately, Dr. Doe could admit that it wasn't just about money. There was a certain intimacy to surgery. Seeing the inside of someone like that.

Dr. Doe was a virgin in his 40s. Probably because he spent so much time doing surgery. He spent so much time in surgery because he was a virgin.

A snake eats its own tail and comes to Dr. Doe looking for someone to remove a foreign object lodged in its throat. Later, it returns to Dr. Doe hoping to get a tail transplant.

"I need you to open me up," John says to Dr. Doe. "I need you to find my soul."

"What?"

"I need you to find my soul. It's for an exhibit. At The Arthouse. Have you heard of it?"

"No. I find galleries pretentious."

"Okay. I still want you to do it, even if you think it's pretentious. To cut me open and find my soul. Will you?"

"I won't find it. I'll find just your intestines. And your liver. And the fat on your liver."

"How do you know there's fat on my liver?"

"You're an artist, aren't you? And a failed one at that. So you drink, don't you?"

"I do."

"Drinking makes your liver fatty. That's how I know. So, I'll find your liver fat. But I won't find a soul. There won't be one, I'm telling you."

"For my life's savings, for all my assets. For The Arthouse. The building itself and all it contains, would you *try* to find my soul?"

And for no other reason than the fact he'd recently lost his job, Dr. Doe agrees.

The gallery is set-up less like an art gallery and more like a slaughterhouse or an operating theater. Makeshift seating has been built on gentle slopes, like a black box theater. All of the frames are empty. As they look for the soul, John's organs will be placed in those frames. It's part of the art; it's part of the search. There's an operating bed with restraints, a metal bucket for excess viscera, and a metal dish full of tools. There's an audience. There's tension thick in the air. Bated breaths. What is art except for self-mutilating violence with an audience?

It's time to bear his soul. It's time to make art.

John is under the strongest painkillers that money can buy, but he's insisted on being awake until the end. Hence the restraint. If he struggled too much, they'll never find the soul.

They start looking for the soul in the intestines. All they find is blood and partially digested food.

"I told you," says the doctor. "You're not going to find it."

"I have to."

They look for it in the heart next.

"No," says John. "Too much blood. Look somewhere else."

"If I cut open your brain, you'll die."

"It's not in the brain."

"I don't wanna look for the soul in your dick."

"It's not *there.*"

"We're running out of places to look."

John wiggles his fingers where they're in the cuffs.

"Sure," says Dr. Doe.

So they try the hands. Dr. Doe carefully runs the scalpel from the base of John's palm to the tip of his middle finger. He pulls the tendons out, one by one.

John tries to wiggle his fingers but finds he cannot. He can no longer make art; he is art. He can no longer make; he is.

"There it is," John whispers, reverent.

"This isn't the soul," Dr. Doe says, carrying one of the tendons to one of the empty frames.

"Yes, it is. There it is. Oh my *God.*"

John then goes into shock and dies, as one does when visiting an art house.

The DCC – Addison Fulton (she/her)

Incandescent bulbs buzz like flies. Have you ever noticed that? It's one of those things that's been on Alex's mind lately, all of the things that sound like bugs if you're paying attention.

The lights, for example. The rattling of some loose part of their car's engine that clicks like the mandibles of a beetle. Overcooked pasta, with its squelching sound like maggots. Their heartbeat, thrumming less like a fly and more like a moth, desperate for the flame.

"Next!"

They stand, wiping their sweaty palms against their jeans and swallowing. They're hungry; they meant to eat before they left, but they were running late this morning and forgot. Then they'd sat in a waiting room and got hungrier, listening to lights.

They step into a small office with lights identical to those in the hallway. They sit down at a desk opposite a man in a thin yellow tie and a blue badge with yellow lettering reading *DCC* pinned to his breast pocket. Behind him is that poster of a white cat dangling from a tree, holding on by a paw. The poster reads *Hang in there!*

"What can I do for you today?"

"I was hoping to join the donors list for the DCC."

"Okay! Okay, that's great. We're always needing more people willing to donate their bodies."

On the desk is a small, golden, plastic trophy. The inscription reads *Best Employee.* Next to it is a DCC coffee cup: blue, with yellow lettering. The cup is full of pens, not coffee.

"Yeah."

"Now, the Department of Consensual Cannibalism gets a bad reputation. But it's always creepy thinking about what happens to you after you die. I mean, would you rather be eaten by worms? At least now you're helping your fellow man."

"Are you a body donor?"

"I am," he presses a couple of keys on the computer, then grabs one of the pens and twirls it between his fingers.

"Do you ever... think about it?"

Their mouth goes dry as they ask. They think about the wriggling of worms. They think about being the meatball on someone else's pasta.

"No, not really. The job keeps me busy."

"You'd think a job like this would make you think about it all the time."

"Well, I mean... I think about the Department of Consensual Cannibalism all the time, but I don't really think about *myself.* On the clock, at least."

The longer they look at it, the more terrified the cat on the poster looks. They wonder if it's a body donor.

"Oh."

"Before you can officially join the registry, we need to do some paperwork. Is that alright?"

"Yeah. I got all day."

They do, in fact, have all day. They were recently laid off. That's part of why they were doing this. To be a part of something bigger, sure, but there were benefits. Scholarships. Discounts. Sweepstakes.

"Alright—" he leans over and grabs a stack of papers off of the printer, licks his finger, and flips through them.

"What's your full legal name?"

"Alex Shepherd"

"Alright. Date of birth?"

"October 19th, 2033."

"Okay. And today's date is—" he trails off, clicking his tongue as he looks at his watch and makes a note. "August 27th, 2054. Awesome."

There's more paper shuffling.

"Have you been exposed to prion-disease-carrying animals such as cows or deer in the past three months?"

"I've never seen a cow. Or a deer," their father had seen a cow. He told them they weren't all they were cracked up to be. They were huge and powerful, but they smelled like shit and constantly had flies buzzing in their eyes. Now most industrial farming was done behind closed, smoggy, doors. But even that was falling out of style. It'd gotten expensive to raise meat cows when humans were already raising themselves for free.

"Have you ever had a fungal infection that lasted more than 6 months or required emergency medical attention?"

"No."

"Have you ever been diagnosed with a bloodborne disease, such as Hepatitis?"

"No."

"Have you been diagncsed with diabetes?"

"No."

"Hormonal imbalances?"

"No."

"High blood pressure?"

"No."

"High blood *sugar?*"

"No."

"Self-mutilating thoughts or suicidal ideation?"

"...No."

"Has your primary physician indicated to you that you would be a good candidate for consumption post-mortem?"

"Yes."

"Okay. Well, that's that part over."

"Alright."

"Are you nervous?"

"No. I mean... maybe. A little. I didn't think this would... feel like this, I guess."

"It's okay to be nervous. I was nervous."

"Okay."

"Well, even if you're not nervous, the department has some prepared remarks for people registering to be body donors for the Department of Consensual Cannibalism. It's kind of long, but legally, I have to read it to you."

"Okay."

"Okay," he clears his throat and takes on a strange, somewhat altered tone of voice.

"Thank you for volunteering with the Department of Consensual Cannibalism. Your body is valuable to us. We understand that this, like any confrontation with death, can be an unsettling process for some. We would like to restate: You are safe. Your body is valuable to us. You will be treated with the utmost care. Our staff of doctors and culinary scientists are the brightest minds in the nation.

We would like to clear up some misconceptions about the DCC. Firstly, in no major world religion is being *eaten* a sin, and donating your body to the DCC will not prohibit you from getting into the afterlife of your choosing.

You are not less likely to be helped in the event of an emergency due to a conspiratorial governmental effort to harvest your body sooner.

You will save countless lives and fill countless hearts and stomachs with your body. It is one of the most noble things you can do and the best way to live after death."

He stares at the paper for a moment longer, then whips off his glasses and blinks, shaking himself. When he sets the paper down, he sets it face down.

"Okay! That's my spiel. Any questions?"

"Nope."

"Alright. Well, we're almost done. I just need to get you to sign some consent forms."

He hands over a clipboard with a thin packet of papers with small boxes for initials and one of those blue pens with the yellow lettering down the side: *DCC.*

"You understand that, upon your demise, your body will be used as sustenance for other humans."

"I understand."

"You understand that, should you choose to become a body donor with the Department of Consensual Cannibalism, your next of kin will have to forgo traditional end-of-life rituals, such as viewings, wakes, burials, funerals, cremations, etc."

"I understand."

"You understand that, unlike organ donation, consent to this process is final, and cannot be revoked, by yourself, by next of kin, or by an individual granted power of attorney."

"I understand."

"Lots of people get scared about that part, but it's important. It's how the government tracks the reserves and determines rations. That's why."

"I get it."

"You can keep the pen if you want to."

"Thanks."

"Now this last part is optional, you can choose not to do it, but if you're willing, we have a little exit survey we like donors to do. Helps us understand our demographics."

"Sure. Why not?"

"On a scale of one to ten, one being extremely negative, and ten being extremely positive, how was your perception of the Department of Consensual Cannibalism, *prior* to your first meeting with us?"

"I don't know. A seven? I guess."

"Okay. And on a scale of one to ten, one being extremely negative, and ten being extremely positive, how was your perception of the Department of Consensual Cannibalism, *after* your first meeting with us?"

"8? 8.5?"

"I'll take it. How did you first hear about the donation program with the DCC?"

"In school."

"Have you ever engaged in consensual cannibalism?"

"Yes."

"What made you decide to be a DCC donor?"

"I wish it was for some awesome, noble reason like I just loved humanity so much that I could just get eaten by them and keep them living and then my life would have a purpose. But honestly? It's because funerals are expensive and I don't want my family to have to deal with that. And there are a lot of school scholarships that are only available to meat donors. So that's why. I'm sorry. I wish it were better."

"Don't be ashamed," he says, with a gentle smile. "That's actually a common answer."

He pauses for a moment again, swallowing around nothing.

"A really common answer. Okay, last question. If you could eat anything in the world right now, what would it be?"

"Cheesecake, probably. With whipped cream. And a cherry," they hadn't had cherries since they were a child still living with their parents. There was no way they could afford cherries on their current budget.

"Good one. Well, I can't offer that, but because you became a body donor today, I *can* offer you this gift card. It's to the burger place across the street."

"Do they use human meat?"

"...*Yeah*... But! For an upcharge, you can get beef."

"Cool."

"Okay! Is there anything else we can help you with? We can also help with voter registration, driver's licenses, etc."

"I'm good. Thanks."

"Okay! Well, have a good one."

"Thanks. You too."

They do end up going to the burger place for dinner and paying the beef upcharge, only because they had the gift card. The meat is saltier and juicier than human. It has cheese that melts like hot glue.

It's delicious.

Pretty Poison – Chriss Locker (they/them)

The first cigarette was the best.

Pilfered from the depths of his mother's purse while she slept away yet another day, it made his thirteen-year-old heart race hands shake blood pound head swimspin*fly*.

The first cigarette made him run for a second-third-fourth-fifth in a row until he couldn't breathe, couldn't *breathe*, couldn't couldn't couldn't

stand any longer, and he vomited into the grass before collapsing, and when his mother found him sometime after sunset, she laughed.

-

A pack a day soon became two packs a day, soon became a few pills here and a joint or three there, but it was never enough, never fucking enough to make him gasp like that first cigarette, to send him over the edge and into that oblivious ecstasy until it was an entire pot of coffee to get him out of bed in the morning, and a line of coke to get him to school, and another couple lines to propel him through lunch and to evening, when he was finally free to run home and crash with the aid of a few shots of whiskey or some codeine or whatever else he could get his hands on.

It was substances and sleep and days that blurred into nights that blurred into concerned glances swirling colors aching shaking hollow/hollow/hollow heart head lungs belly *soul*.

-

And not enough became too much with no warning no escape no light nonononothing.

No job.

No food.

No sleep.

No school.

No friends.

Nothing.
Nothing.
Nothing.

-

Needles.   Powder.   Pills.

Blood.   Sweat.   Vomit.

Nothing.   Nothing.   Nothing.

-

It was blue eyes and cold hands and that voice—his voice—
screaming/crying, *please no please don't God damn it
wakeupwakeupWAKEUP.*

It was white sheets with white walls with white dreams. Tubes and
wires and more needles and more pills.

It was Ellis sobbing, Ellis stroking his cheeks while he
sleptfloated*flew*, Ellis pleading with him...

Don't you dare *leave me.*

-

Breathing.	Stirring.	Waking.
Holding.	Kissing.	Crying.
Sorry.	Sorry.	Sorry.

-

Something.

Twice – Sarp Sozdinler (he/him)

After today, they may say that I lived as I died: twice.

Some superficial people may think that just because I died once, I couldn't live twice. Or that I've lived twice should mean I was born twice. Neither could be any further from the truth. Let's be fair and say I was born (once) in the wetlands of Florida thanks to the skillful hands of a midwife; was killed (once) in the wet sands of California by the fast hands of two friends; and was revived (once) by the wet lips of a lifeguard, who vacuumed those sands out of my lungs.

That's why I pick the most arid, unpeopled place I know on Earth to die for a second and, hopefully, the last time—drily and lonely—and climbed on the roof of an abandoned soap factory in the middle of Nevada.

Yet, only a few minutes into my suicide attempt, the sky growls and splits into a downpour as if to grieve me beforehand. To my luck, or lack thereof, a girl who is half my age and twice my size turns out to be squatting the place I was about to jump.

"Man, you need to stop crying," she says as soon as she spots me, mistaking the undried slits of rain on my eyelids for tears. She turns the safety off on the gun she's pointing at me. "It makes you look fat."

The first time I died was three years ago when my friends buried me at the beach for fun. We were just done with the second round of having laps in the Florida Panhandle and ready for some leisurely time. I lay flat on my Bob Marley towel like a beached baby whale and watched them cover me with sand until my body resembled a newly dug grave. Well, let me be frank and admit that there is no way I could know about what happened post-mortem. The details in-between are all fuzzy now, like watching a color film on a dim TV. One moment I was counting the yellow birds circling above the waves, and the next thing I knew my complexion was matching the purple sheets of a hospital bed, next to an older patient whose eyes were the icy white of a corpse.

After I woke up though, I remember that my lips looked so blue and dehydrated that I had to apply aloe vera moisturizers for weeks to come—twice a day. White-headed blisters freckled the vicinity of my oral cavity like some dead astronauts floating in outer space.

Which kept me thinking: what shape would my face have taken had my stay on the other side lasted for another two minutes?

"Just so you know, I don't personally mind you ending me or anything," I say to the rooftop girl who seems to hold the gun with less determination now. "If that's going to make you feel better." I lean over the railings to picture the shapes my body may take once I hit the walkway below. "I mean, I'm dead anyway."

For how it all sounds, some people may take me for a defeatist. Or assume that I lack the willpower. Or if nothing else, that I might have lost a marble or two, considering the scene and conditions of my currently morbid affair. Once again, none of it could be more untrue. Believe it or not, I had previously been the incurable optimist. The pragmatic dreamer. Mind you, for three years now, I've been trying hard not to die. Okay, let's be fair and say, *trying hard to survive*. Sometimes with others. By helping those who wish to die by telling them how nothing happens on the other side. How dying is like trying to cover a void with another one. A vain kinship with the perfect nothingness of life.

Until earlier this morning.

Until the front camera of my smartphone took an accidental selfie at the only spot of my apartment with a decent social media light. Though the sunblock was right for my complexion, what I saw on the screen didn't live up to my expectations. Whatever you name it: a malevolent force, a suborbital stench of mediocrity, some molehill of rot that settled in my foundation three years ago and has since become a mountain.

This morning, my face looked just like when I died the first time.

Blotches populated my discriminatively white cheeks and my twin chin that cascaded like the topographic charts of Nevada. My eyes were shut into a line. Ears were swallowed by the backlight. An idea of a haircut crowded the top of my head, with the inch of blondish white regrowth drawing a horseshoe shape.

All in all, that grim look of a forty-year-old, heralding a worse decade.

"That's all right," the rooftop girl says to me, cracking a walnut with one hand while holding the gun at me with the other. "Just tell me how much you've got on you."

"Just a few hundred, I guess," I say, then remove my wallet from my pants pocket to throw it in her direction. "You can take it all afterward if you like. I don't really care."

Afterward.

That incident on the beach was the first time I died but wasn't my first near-death experience. It happened when I was five; when my mother parked her Forc Bronco by the curbside of a male co-worker's house and absentmindedly told me to wait for her while she handled "this very quick errand," furiously texting someone in the meantime. As I found cut *afterward,* she wouldn't come back for the next four and a half hours. Vehicular heatstroke, the doctors said. Near articular autolysis. Locked in the blistering anguish of a car. Locked out thanks to a concerned carjacker. So said the press. So said the social workers who talked to the press. So said my future foster parents.

In my experience, my breath had gone out almost immediately. I didn't see it coming (or should I say, "going?"). One second I was counting the yellow cars whizzing along the blacktop, and the next thing I knew I was surrounded by an army of nurses and doctors, next to an older kid who was bandaged all over. As I would soon realize, I was in no better shape myself, having had severe sunburns and a more severe heartbreak, coupled with, once again, the extensive signs of dehydration around my lips and tongue.

"Why didn't you just climb out?" asks the rooftop girl—it turns out I've been thinking it all aloud. "Were you one of those kids who couldn't even roll a goddam window without parental help?"

I look her over from head to toe.

"You know those old cars have, like, manual handles, right?" she adds.

I shrug. "Girl, I was only five."

"Bitch, could I get into other people's houses when I was five, let alone get out."

I consider this, nodding into space. "Then how'd you end up here with me today?"

She, too, seems to get lost in her thoughts. "Well," she says, then cracks another walnut. "I guess because I couldn't stop getting into other people's houses once I was five."

The rain stops, and the sun returns.

"So, what is it gonna be?" I ask, eyeing her gun. "Will you end me or let me end myself?"

"I think I'll spare you the decision," she says.

I pout with a shrug and lean forward to measure the odds one last time.

"Or we can leave it to the hands of fate," she adds, and the lines on her face take their time to find their meaning. "A duel or a coin flip. Done for hundreds of years with success. What do you say?"

"But what if I chose the duel and you died?" I ask.

"I wouldn't mind," she says.

"I think I would, but that's okay if you're sure."

She opens her backpack and tosses in my direction a handgun identical to hers, though for some reason it looks larger in my hands.

"I think I'd like to switch back to a coin flip," I say. "I have small hands.”

A beam of sunlight creeps along her face like a forming thought. “Or we can do it both ways,” she offers. “Point our guns at each other and then flip the coin to determine who fires first. Would be more civilized. More gentlewomanly.”

I consider my options for a while. “Please remind me why we don’t simply end ourselves and get it over with,” I ask.

She takes a coin out of her pants pocket and settles it on the curve of her thumb. “Because whoever survives gets to tell a fine story.”

I nod compliantly. Then watch her flip the coin.

Delivery – Victoria Hood (she/her)

My new ghost is coming today. My email buzzed with the news that my money was not a waste, that they sent it after all, that finally it will be arriving, it is out for delivery. I remember the day I bought it, it was just yesterday. I was sad and stoned, all alone thinking of things I didn't have, sad and soggy with emotion. There is something so lonely about a house with objects that are never new. There is something sloppy and sad about living with objects, always gifts from others, never quite what you wanted. *You need more ghosts*, I said, *what is a house without ghosts?*

I moved recently. So recently my house is mostly boxes and frustrations. Objects sorted by room and feeling. Objects that began being sorted through use, but at some point it always just ends up getting sorted by vibe, sorted by the things I touch most, sorted by what I felt like looking at. I slapped labels on the boxes: livingroom, kitchen, bedroom. None of the labels matter. No one needs a whisk in their bedroom.

I am not sure how things work when you buy a ghost. I'm not sure how they ship—could it fit in one of those bubbly envelopes? I've always thought it would be the best way to travel. Oh, I just hope they didn't use packing peanuts. They get everywhere. Inside my ghost, on my floor, somehow always in the toilet. Does the ghost come with its shell? Does it detach from its past? Will it know it's for sale? If there was an upgrade to lifelong friend then I would have splurged for a ghost that was friends with me since we were little—or at least a ghost that *thought* we were friends since we were little. Of course, this is a package I need to sign for.

My new ghost is coming in just an hour, the clock on the delivery ticks away, singing a song every five minutes that passes (that was an upcharge, of course, but if you're waiting then you might as well wait in style). My new ghost will hopefully help me unpack. My new ghost will hopefully be friendly and fun and all the things I never seem to be. My new ghost will be my best friend, that is why I chose this ghost. Right off the menu, I pointed and clicked and sent them my money—plastic for ghost. This is what the menu read: Ghost number 3078 is afraid of heights and ducks, enjoys picnics and bike rides, refuses to eat snow cones, and died of death 184 years ago. *Wow,* I remember thinking, *what an old soul.*

I picture my new ghost tall and plump. Like a friend that I always want to hug. I picture my new ghost all happiness so I hid all of my ducks. At some point everyone needs to make a decision for what will truly bring them happiness—I decided ghost. My sister chose carrots and my brother chose trolls—sometimes we just have to decide.

There are so many questions I have for my ghosts, but the website says to start off easy—like a cat they say. Let them get to know their surroundings, let them mull around and scratch your furniture, let them know they're home. I made their favorite: sandwiches.

The website also says to keep your microwave off for at least a week after they arrive (and not to plug it in without telling them). Toast, the website recommends, toast and toast and toast until you don't have any more and then maybe go to the store and get enough toast for your ghost, be a good owner. I checked the FAQ visa vee the toast and it only says to trust the process. I want to be a good owner, possibly the best owner, I want to drown my ghost with love and happiness and maybe even tell it all my secrets, have sleepovers, picnics in the park, picnics in my backyard, picnics at my neighbors. I checked the FAQ, to be more informed, but the answers always feel more like questions than directions. Q: "How does one care for your ghost?" A: "Like you would a good friend, a living friend, like if you died and someone bought you." Q: "Where does your business procure your ghosts?" A: "The morgue." Q: "How many ghosts should a household have?" A: "How many ghosts do you want?"

I wonder if living with death will make me feel more or less alive. I wonder about the people who buy ghosts, people like me who didn't want the responsibility of caring too hard. I wonder if they're more work than a cat, or more work than a fish, I was expecting a rock. Rocks don't eat picnics, I remind myself, it couldn't have been a rock.

I wonder if it's too late to cancel, the clock is almost at zero. I wonder if I ghost proofed my house enough—I put up extra walls to keep an active hunting mindset. I wonder if that is them in my driveway pulling up. I hear the song play on my phone one last time: "Ooooo, we're here."

NON FICTION

Work Trip – Rachel Wagner (she/her)

I got this book in Birmingham called *Vox*.

I got it because the cover was pink. I decided while walking around this antique store slash bookstore that pink books are usually good girly fun. I came to that conclusion after coming down one isle, reading over a couple hundred titles in brown and grey and black. Skimming along, stepping alone. I was out there for a conference but I always take time away to do my favorite things.

I love being in used bookstores and looking at everything. It's like a museum opening, like performance art where you are the one gliding up and down narrow walkways. Bumping and looking at others doing the same. It's so quiet and internal. You can hear a person asking for a certain version of a cookbook up ahead. One time, years ago, I had this guy take me to a low budget performance of *Macbeth* that was taking place in a library nearby. The players slipped between the stacks to step off stage. Peeking behind aisles, I remember a girl smiled at me on her way around.

That afternoon in Alabama, I passed rows and rows of books. Some books you can't even see because they're behind others. Or else they're piled on the floor in a way that makes it uncomfortable to bend over them. You have to just hope that there's nothing good back there. The Alabama section was cool but I kept with what I knew—an orange June Jordan book looking like an oversized starburst. Saw that early on. Didn't even have to read the title, I knew I was going to get it because her name was written across it.

Then down some more I landed on the pink book theory when I found *Vox*. Didn't know what that word meant but I saw it was a sexual, erotic, pussy pink novel. *Okay yea.*

Read one page later on my hotel bed but I traveled home to Jersey finishing something else because I simply couldn't take on something new. I was wiped out from the trip and the presentation and the writing and the traveling and the preparation and the editing and the slight neck injury I acquired earlier that fateful week. I was dying tired. Felt dehydrated trying to participate in the conference, but I tried. Took showers all the time. Laid down in my bed naked at every spare moment. That was how I recharged. Slipping into cold white sheets at the Sheraton.

I walked out the store with the books in a bag and walked on in search of food and other things to look at. I walked and walked. It felt good. Not even knowing I was walking where MLK once moved. I came to this Baptist church on 16th street not knowing it was The 16th Street Baptist Church. I sat on the steps seemingly alone until a group of kids came bursting through the door below. Something drew me there maybe it was the whole setup of the park. You do kinda follow the statues after you're done eating your fried chicken and stuff. Walked around a lot more and eventually sat down at this lil' mini corner park waiting for a ride back.

But the drivers down there take fifteen minutes minimum to show up. So I sat on the bench a while and when I look up, this dude sitting in his car is asking me where this certain food place is at, the one I just ate at. The one direction I can give! But really he already knew. He just said that to then say to come by him and take his number down. Cute ways, sweet smile. I remember standing there with the sun shining right in his eye. It was a day that had already changed from cool to warm. I was holding my coat and everything and he's talking about he wanna see me later. But I had to go and there just wasn't time and we didn't get to see each other but now we're just on the phone all the time.

I'm reading *Vox* at home and I'm talking to the dude and he's cool and the book is good. In the story, there's no he said she said, it's just straight dialogue. Two people talking on a sex hotline. And they offer to each other about 1/3 of the way in to hang up and call off their regular phones, but they decide against it because it might mess up the magic. They might not have the same tone so even though it was costing him however much per minute, he was like whatever I'll pay it. Meanwhile me and this Alabama dude are talking every day. All day, texting, FaceTiming, all different ways. We like each other we're like *damn why you gotta be so far away.* We wanna see each other. We hang up all the time and it's no problem because it's about the act of calling back that's appealing.

Ah fate. When two people both crush. I was utterly obsessionless like two seconds ago with no one to even dream about or want or need at night. I was good, I was bored, I was single as a dollar bill. I was not even looking forward to meeting anyone of any sort ever again. I accepted that it's garbage out here and I could choose not to participate. Then, now, here I am smiling and rereading messages in my down time. Laughing and saying *I like you so much* and wishing I never left, wishing I could come back this second, wanting to know how he feels. Who he is in person.

The couple in *Vox* openly talk about other people. It's not necessarily about them. It's about times they masturbated around another person and other little mini relationships they've been in. A circus fantasy or these long arms someone had. Trying to get a photocopy of his dick or touching herself in the shower in college. Relating through their sexual past slash fantasy. And the narrator doesn't know anything. There are no physical descriptions or internal thoughts or raised eyebrows.

All that's there is what is said.

A Thursday in November – Adenah Furquan (she/her)

It is on a Thursday in November that I learn why I was made. Autumn is in full swing, its kaleidoscope of reds and greens enveloping me whole. I feel the heat from the fireplace caress my skin and I wonder if life has always been this simple. The answer comes to me like tea falling from a pot: slow and gentle, fused with the rousing rush of something promising.

An old friend texts to tell me she misses me and I cry for the first time in weeks. On paper this is a simple act requiring no more than a couple seconds. But, as with all matters of the heart, it quickly consumes my entire being. Another friend calls to ask about my favorite books. An hour later a stack of Dostoevsky sits still at my doorstep.

In the kitchen, my mother peels a basket's worth of persimmons for me, filling the room with the sort of saccharine scent that only motherhood can bring. My grandmother prays for my *achay naseeb* (good fate), her eyes so tender you could swim in the pools of their warmth. I like to call myself a writer, but I don't think the words have ever escaped me quicker. I can only describe it all as transcendental.

Do you know what it's like to be remembered like this? With intent and not reluctance? Without starving and pleading for it? To be thought of like this, in the form of a prayer even, is this not the greatest thing to have happened to me? I am not sure what to do with all that you've given me, but I promise you I will not refuse. It is the least I can do for you.

And if I could keep anything it would be this. The moonlight dancing across our skin. The laughter resounding through this room. Your hair falling over your forehead. My hands having their own memory. It's hard not to think I'm immortal when life looks like this. It's even harder not to believe in love. It is all— and has always been—for love.

ABOUT THE CONTRIBUTORS

- ❖ Abu Ibrahim popularly known as IB is a Nigerian poet whose work has had tremendous influence. Some of his works have also been published in literary outfits in Canada, the United States, the United Kingdom, and more. He reads for Fahmidan.

- ❖ Addison Fulton was born and raised in Albuquerque, New Mexico on the most beautiful sunsets. She has deep roots, like everything that grows in the desert. She believes all of life can be sorted into the following categories: the beautiful, the grotesque, and the mundane. In her work, she seeks to create art that exists at the intersection of all three. She has previously been published in the literary magazines, *Homer Humanities*, *Scribendi* and in the short story anthology *Pretty Obscure*. She has a series of urban-fantasy thriller novels titled Social Animals, debuting in 2024 with Far West Press.

- ❖ Adenah Furquan (she/her) is a Pakistani American with an earnest passion for writing and feminism. When she's not brainstorming ideas for new pieces or trying to dismantle the patriarchy, Adenah can be found listening to indie rock, reading old literature, and gushing over scented candles with a bowl of tiramisu in her hand.

- ❖ Adonis Alegre (he/him) was a college writer and language graduate at Don Mariano Marcos Memorial State University. His poems have appeared or forthcoming in *Levitate Magazine*, *The Mluc Voice,* and *Nightshade Lit Mag*. He lives in Bacnotan and currently works as an intern in the government sector.

- ❖ Alexander Beets (he/him) is a Puerto Rican writer from Roanoke Rapids, North Carolina. He is pursuing an M.A in Creative Writing at UNC Charlotte. A lot of his work involves exploring the intersections and effects of the industrialism and classicism that has grown and evolved in rural North Carolina, and what that looks like for the people still living there. You can find some of his older work in Nova Literary-Arts Magazine and Carolina Muse.

- ❖ Ann Kammerer (she/her) lives in Oak Park, Illinois, having recently moved from her home state of Michigan with her husband and daughter. Her fiction and poetry have appeared in *Fictive Dream, One Art, Open Arts Forum, Bright Flash Literary Review, Thoughtful Dog,* and *Ekphrastic Review,* among others, and anthologies by Crow Woods Publishing and Querencia Press. She has received top honors and made the short list in several writing competitions. Her chapbook collections of narrative poetry include "Yesterday's Playlist" (Bottlecap Press, 2023), "Beaut" (Kelsay Books, 2024), and "Friends Once There" (Impspired, 2024). You can find her here: www.annkammerer.com

- ❖ Antonia Rachel Ward is an author of horror and speculative fiction, based in Cambridgeshire, UK. Her short stories and poetry have been published by Flame Tree Press, the British Science Fiction Association, and Dark Recesses, among others. She is the author of two novellas, *Marionette* and *Attack of the Killer Tumbleweeds*, and her first novel, *DreamScape*, was published in October 2023. Her first poetry chapbook, *The Patron*, is forthcoming from Querencia Press in 2024. She is also the founder and editor-in-chief of Ghost Orchid Press.

❖ Archie J. is a queer and trans-man poet from the Southern, USA. His writing often involves themes of growing up within this environment, devotion, and deep love, with an overall Southern Gothic theme in most works. His favorite time to write is early in the morning or late in the evening. When not writing poetry, you can find him curled up with his dog reading horror novels and drinking a cup of hot tea.

❖ Ariya Bandy (she/her) is a writer of fiction and poetry whose debut poetry chapbook, Painted Winds, is out from Bottlecap Press. Her work appears in Stone Circle Review, The Horror Tree, anthologies from Querencia Press, and elsewhere.

❖ Camille is a Black, Queer Fem, Mama & Writer based in San Francisco, California. Her work has appeared with the Black Femme Collective, on Cafe Mom, Mixed Mag & Variety Pack. A mainly creative non-fiction writer, she spends just as much time with poetry. She has a cat named Gloom and pours cinnamon on everything. Find her at www.camillecolpitts.com

❖ Cat Speranzini (she/her) is a native New Englander and Emerson college alumna. Her first full length poetry collection, "Watercolor Souls," was released January 2024. Her work also appears in the Eunoia Review and FUCKUS Lit Mag.

❖ Chriss Locker (they/them) is a nonbinary, neurodivergent poet living in Northern Idaho with their spouse, cat, dog, and too many unused college degrees. Healthcare professional by day. Daydreamer by night. Look for their work in issue three of *new words* from new words {press}, the debut issue of *Tension Literary, and milk: on consumption, materialism, and taste* from Carrion Press. You can follow them on Instagram @viciouschrisss.

❖ Damon Hubbs writes poems about Thulsa Doom, Italo disco & girls who cry at airports. He's the author of two chapbooks (most recently *Coin Doors & Empires*, from Alien Buddha Press). Recent work appears/is forthcoming in *A Thin Slice of Anxiety, Red Ogre Review, Broken Antler, Dreich, Voidspace, Riggwelter Press*, & elsewhere. twitter @damon_hubbs

❖ Daniel Lockendge (he/him) is a twenty-nine-year-old Australian who has self-published two collections of poetry and two collections of meditative reminders. His poetry has been published in literary magazines such as The Winged Moon Magazine, Reverie Magazine, Free Verse Revolution, Livina Press and Boats against the Current, among others. He also shares poems and loving reminders on his Instagram page: @danlovepoetry.

❖ Diane Elayne Dees (she/her) is the author of the chapbooks, *Coronary Truth* (Kelsay Books), *The Last Time I Saw You* (Finishing Line Press) and *The Wild Parrots of Marigny* (Querencia Press). She is also the author of four Origami Poems Project microchaps, and her poetry, short fiction and creative nonfiction have been published in many journals and anthologies. Diane, who lives in Covington, Louisiana—just across Lake Pontchartrain from New Orleans—also publishes Women Who Serve, a blog that delivers news and commentary on women's professional tennis throughout the world. Her author blog is Diane Elayne Dees: Poet and Writer-at-Large.

❖ Elizabeth Adan is probably weaving words together right now. A lifelong writer and artist who enjoys deconstructing the smallest moments and largest emotions, often at the same time, her alliterative, lyrical writing takes on topics ranging from sustainability, nature, love lost/found, and community responsibility. A Pacific Northwest native, her true passion is the great outdoors, soaking up as much inspiration and natural color as possible.
Find Elizabeth on Instagram and Twitter @edgeofelizabeth or at www.ElizabethAdanArt.squarespace.com.

❖ Elle Jay Snyder (she/her/hers) is a transwoman, poet, and part-time phantom from Staten Island. She has represented her borough as part of the 2018 Advanced Slam Team at NPS, facilitated workshops in her community and for LGBTQIA youth, buried herself alive at Queer Van Kult: Revelation exhibition in 2022, and published a limited release chapbook, Where the Knife Landed, from NYSAI Press. Her work has appeared in several anthologies from great weather for Media Press, Lupercalia Press, In Between Hangovers, et. al. Her work is forthcoming in the anthology, When Flowers Sing, from A thousand flowers Press. She is also aggressively seeking a sponsorship from Mountain Dew.

❖ Emily Drez (she/her) has a BA in English from Louisiana State University. She has been writing stories in beat-up notebooks since she was six years old, and she lives in Baton Rouge where she writes, reads, and teaches about reading and writing.

❖ Emma Wells is a mother and English teacher. She has poetry published with various literary journals and magazines. She writes flash fiction, short stories and novels. She is currently writing her fifth novel. Emma won Wingless Dreamer's Bird Poetry Contest of 2022 with 'Carbonito de Sophie' and her short story entitled 'Virginia Creeper' was selected as a winning title by WriteFluence Singles Contest in 2021. Recently, she won Dipity Literary Magazine's 2024 Best of the Net Nominations for Fiction with her short story entitled 'The Voice of a Wildling'.

❖ *Fern (they/them+she/her)* writes and teaches experimental poetry*, between mutual aid and long-distance hiking. They have tutored and mc'd Open Mics at the Evergreen Writing Center, and their work has appeared in the Cultivating Voices Pride Poetry March, Slightly West, The Cooper Point Journal, and the Mobile Moon Coop Zine. Find her-- and the SEEJSanctuary Crew-- at moonlitfern.com ***hint**: it's all poetry.

❖ Frances Klein (she/her) is an Alaskan poet and teacher. She is the 2022 winner of the Robert Golden Poetry Prize. Klein is the author of several poetry chapbooks, including "(Text) Messages from The Angel Gabriel" (Gnashing Teeth Press, 2024). Her full length collection Another Life is forthcoming from Riot in Your Throat Press in 2025. Klein's writing has appeared or is forthcoming in The Harvard Advocate, The Atticus Review, HAD, and others.

❖ Grant Shimmin (he/him) is a South African-born poet living in New Zealand. Humanity, nature, and their relationship are poetic passions. He has work published/forthcoming at Roi Faineant Press, Does it Have Pockets?, The

Hooghly Review, underscore_magazine, Remington Review, Epistemic Lit and elsewhere.

* Irina Tall (Novikova) is an artist, graphic artist, illustrator. She graduated from the State Academy of Slavic Cultures with a degree in art, and also has a bachelor's degree in design. The first personal exhibition "My soul is like a wild hawk" (2002) was held in the museum of Maxim Bagdanovich. In her works, she raises themes of ecology, in 2005 she devoted a series of works to the Chernobyl disaster, draws on anti-war topics. The first big series she drew was The Red Book, dedicated to rare and endangered species of animals and birds. Writes fairy tales and poems, illustrates short stories. She draws various fantastic creatures: unicorns, animals with human faces, she especially likes the image of a man - a bird - Siren. In 2020, she took part in Poznań Art Week. Her work has been published in magazines: Gupsophila, Harpy Hybrid Review, Little Literary Living Room and others. In 2022, her short story was included in the collection "The 50 Best Short Stories", and her poem was published in the collection of poetry "The wonders of winter".

* Jess Whetsel (she/her) is a poet, writer, editor, and public speaker based in Toledo, Ohio on Erie Kickapoo, Seneca, and Odawa land. She holds a bachelor's degree in English Writing and German from Denison University, and a Master of Social Work degree from the University of Denver. Her poetry has appeared in several literary journals, including Tulip Tree Review, Discretionary Love, and Sage Cigarettes. She released her first collection of poetry, A SOFTER KIND OF AUDACITY, in December 2023. You can learn more about Whetsel and her work on her website, www.jesswhetsel.com, or by following her Instagram, @jesswhetselwrites.

* Jillian Stacia wants to live in a world where the coffee is bottomless and the sweatpants are mandatory. She spends her days crafting creative copy for clients in numerous industries and is known for her work in Children's Programming. Her poetry and narrative essays have been featured in Remington Review, Coffee & Crumbs, and Gypsophila Zine. When she's not writing, Jillian can be found snuggling with her two adorable children and cheering on the Baltimore Ravens.

* John Chinaka Onyeche is a multi-talented writer. He is a poet, essayist and teacher of African History. He has authored numerous chapbooks and full-length collections of poems such as: "Echoes across the Atlantic," "A Night Tale at the Threshold of Howl," "We Returned to Kiss the Cross," "The Broken Fort," "A Good Day for Tomorrow's Coming," "Stateless," "25 Atonements," "Chapters of Broken Tale," and "The Gathering Of Reeds," (which is scheduled for publication in March, 2024 by Ethel Zine Press), Time & Songs Of The River Men (2024 by warrioresspublishing.com), Symphonies Of Mired Songs (2024 by southernarizonapress.com). His literary prowess has earned him recognition as a Best of Net Nominee 2022, and Pushcart 2023.

* K.H. Belzer (she/her) is an emerging writer from the coast of British Columbia, Canada. Her writing explores mental illness, motherhood and spirituality in its most raw and provocative form: poetry. She is a mother of 3 and currently working on her first poetry collection.

* K Weber (she/her) is an Ohio writer with 10 online books of poetry. She

obtained her Creative Writing BA in 1999 from Miami University. K writes independently and collaboratively, having created poems from words donated by more than 300 people since 2018. K has poems featured in publications such as *The Hooghly Review*, *Writer's Digest*, *Fevers of the Mind* & her photography/digital collages appear in literary journals including *Barren Magazine* and *Nightingale & Sparrow*. Much of K's work (free in PDF and some in audiobook format) and her publishing credits are on her website: kweberandherwords.com

❖ Lizeth De La Luz is a poet from California. She is pursuing an MFA degree at San Francisco State University. She writes about the frustration of language barriers, learned barriers, and the anxieties of living/loving/grieving in a Mexican body in the United States. She is the Senior Field Notes Editor at *Defunkt* magazine. Her work can be found in City Works, Short Vine, and Transfer magazine.

❖ Maggie Bowyer (they/he) is a poet, co-host of the podcast Baked and Bookish, and the author of various poetry collections including *Homecoming* (2023) and *When I Bleed* (2021). They've been published in Chapter House Journal, The South Dakota Review, Wishbone Words, and more. Find their work on Instagram @maggie.writes

❖ Maria Duran (she/her) is a researcher and writer from Lisbon, Portugal. She writes poetry and prose, studies little known nineteenth-century painters and is currently writing a chapbook. Her work has been published with *Helvética Press*, *Gilbert & Hall Press*, *Black Moon Magazine*, *Third Iris Magazine*, *P'Arte* and *Vagabond City Magazine*, and will soon be published with *Pollux Journal* and *Ofélia em Poesia*. Maria Duran (@m.mar.duran) · Instagram.

❖ Mattie-Bretton Hughes is a disabled, nonbinary-transmasc writer from Detroit, Michigan. He is a recovering addict and journals to discover the layers of systemic trauma, identity, body dysphoria, disability, intimate partner violence, and addiction, while exploring the human condition with inspiration from nature and the cosmos. He cares for a blind rescue cat named Mr. Ray Charles Kitty. Mattie's work has appeared in Querencia Press, Beyond The Veil Press, Snowflake Magazine, Wishbone Words, and elsewhere. You can catch him on Instagram @mattiebretton27.

❖ Melanie Hess writes from British Columbia, Canada. Through imagery and vivid detail, Melanie strives to create candid "snapshots" that invite readers into the internal and external landscapes of life and what it means to be human. At a young age she learned the power of words to harm or heal and has spoken out ever since.

❖ Michelle Gerlach is a DJ, self-taught musician and public speaker. She works at Living Studios in Corvallis, Oregon. She was born with Cerebral Palsy and grew up in Florida.

❖ Mirvat Manal is a British/Somali fiction writer & poet based in the UK. Her work has been published in The Leon Literary Review, Maudlin House, Kalahari Review and elsewhere.

❖ M.J.D. Deetzy is an asexual multi-hobbyist who has been diagnosed with depression, major anxiety, and AuDHD. Though when she first found out about these terms, she was wholeheartedly opposed to aligning with them. She was taught that her problems weren't as bad as they could be, therefore invalid. She was often brushed aside from people she should've been able to look up to. So she turned to writing as a form of trying to figure out her mind. Eventually, she learned that being autistic wasn't a synonym to "stupid," or "less than," and learned to be kinder to herself by figuring out triggers and ways to work with her neurodivergent-wired brain. She hopes to prove her mean thoughts wrong, and her past self that she in fact can add good things to this world, and that they can still exist.

❖ Niki is a person who lives in Brighton, UK, at the moment. He owns a bookshelf, a MacBook, boxing gloves, an empty bucket of yogurt, 3 Pokemon cards, lists of things, etc. Through his window, he can see a strangely tall bush—which is more like a tree but still pretty much a bush—which his neighbour downstairs managed to nurture within the confines of a little garden. It looks sad and freezing (the bush)

❖ Rachel Wagner is a writer from New Jersey, currently living in Newark with her son. She teaches first-year writing at Seton Hall University and runs an online bookstore called Ten Dollar Books. More of her work can be found at Rachel-Wagner.com.

❖ Sarah Merrifield (she/they) is a non-binary, lesbian, disabled, and neurodivergent poet who uses her writing to share her journey of working through PTSD. She hopes to serve as an inspiration for others who live with mental illness. She has been published in Querencia Press's Anthology "Not Ghosts, but Spirits Volume II" and Harness Magazine online. .

❖ A writer of Turkish descent, Sarp Sozdinler (he/him) has been published in Electric Literature, Kenyon Review, Masters Review, DIAGRAM, Normal School, Vestal Review, Maudlin House, and American Literary Review, among other places. His stories have been selected or nominated for anthologies (Pushcart Prize, Best of the Net, Best Small Fictions, Wigleaf Top 50) and awarded a finalist status at various literary contests, including the 2022 Los Angeles Review Flash Fiction Award. He's currently at work on his first novel in Philadelphia and Amsterdam."

❖ Victoria Hood (she/her) is the author of a collection of short stories *My Haunted Home* (FC2) and chapbooks *Death and Darlings* and *Entries of Boredom and Fear* (Bottlecap Press). Her book of poetry, *I Am My Mother's Disappointments*, released on Mother's Day 2024 from Girl Noise Press.. She hopes to discomfort, humor, and charm.

OTHER TITLES FROM QUERENCIA

Allison by Marisa Silva-Dunbar

GIRL. by Robin Williams

Retail Park by Samuel Millar

Every Poem a Potion, Every Song a Spell by Stephanie Parent

songs of the blood by Kate MacAlister

Love Me Louder by Tyler Hurula

God is a Woman by TJ McGowan

Learning to Float by Alyson Tait

Fever by Shilo Niziolek

Cutting Apples by Jomé Rain

Girl Bred from the 90s by Olivia Delgado

Wax by Padraig Hogan

When Memory Fades by Faye Alexandra Rose

The Wild Parrots of Marigny by Diane Elayne Dees

Hospital Issued Writing Notebook by Dan Flore III

Knees in the Garden by Christina D Rodriguez

Provocative is a Girl's Name by Mimi Flood

Bad Omens by Jessica Drake-Thomas

Beneath the Light by Laura Lewis-Waters

Ghost Hometowns by Giada Nizzoli

Dreamsoak by Will Russo

the abyss is staring back by nat raum

How Long Your Roots Have Grown by Sophia-Maria Nicolopoulos

The World Eats Butterflies Like You by Isabelle Quilty

Playing Time in Tongues by Vita Lerman

unloving the knife by Lilith Kerr

5 Spirits in My Mouth by Pan Morigan

You Shouldn't Worry About the Frogs by Eliza Marley

Now Let's Get Brunch: A Collection of RuPaul's Drag Race Twitter Poetry by Alex Carrigan

The Dissection of a Tiger by Tyler Walter

Reasons Why We're Angry by Sophia Isabella Murray

An Absurd Palate by Alysa Levi-D'Ancona

9 781963 943078